DEADLY DELIVERY

The ear-splitting crack of the first shot echoed off the surrounding rocks. Fargo felt a sharp tug at his buckskin shirt as the bullet passed harmlessly through the folds of his left armpit. He hit the rocky trail hard, landing on his left shoulder and hip. His Colt was already to hand, but so far he had no target.

The hidden marksman did not let up. Again and again he levered and fired, bullets whanging off the rocks all around Fargo. The well-trained Ovaro began to back down the trail, refusing to run away completely without Fargo.

Fargo traded bullet for bullet as he grabbed the Ovaro's reins and began leading him quickly back down the trail. One round whizzed past so close it damn near parted Fargo's hair, and when it splattered into a boulder, rock dust flew in his eyes.

"Whoever the hell you are, mister," Fargo roared out in a voice powerful enough to fill a canyon, "you just broke the rules! And you tell Danford this: Skye Fargo says he'll never see one red cent of that money if even one kid is hurt. Now we're playing by *my* rules, and you just remember—hell ain't even *half* full. . . ."

THE TRAILSMAN

#262

BADLAND BLOODBATH

by

Jon Sharpe

A SIGNET BOOK

SIGNET
Published by New American Library, a division of
Penguin Group (USA) Inc., 375 Hudson Street,
New York, New York 10014, U.S.A.
Penguin Books Ltd, 80 Strand,
London WC2R 0RL, England
Penguin Books Australia Ltd, 250 Camberwell Road,
Camberwell, Victoria 3124, Australia
Penguin Books Canada Ltd, 10 Alcorn Avenue,
Toronto, Ontario, Canada M4V 3B2
Penguin Books (N.Z.) Ltd, Cnr Rosedale and Airborne Roads,
Albany, Auckland 1310, New Zealand

Penguin Books Ltd, Registered Offices:
80 Strand, London WC2R 0RL, England

First published by Signet, an imprint of New American Library,
a division of Penguin Group (USA) Inc.

First Printing, August 2003
10 9 8 7 6 5 4 3 2 1

The first chapter of this book previously appeared in *Desert Death Trap*,
the two hundred sixty-first volume in this series.

The Trailsman

Beginnings . . . they bend the tree and they mark the man. Skye Fargo was born when he was eighteen. Terror was his midwife, vengeance his first cry. Killing spawned Skye Fargo, ruthless, cold-blooded murder. Out of the acrid smoke of gunpowder still hanging in the air, he rose, cried out a promise never forgotten.

The Trailsman they began to call him all across the West: searcher, scout, hunter, the man who could see where others only looked, his skills for hire but not his soul, the man who lived each day to the fullest, yet trailed each tomorrow. Skye Fargo, the Trailsman, the seeker who could take the wildness of a land and the wanting of a woman and make them his own.

The Badlands, 1861—
Where the Iron Horse carries many to a new life—
and some to a hard death.

1

A hen pheasant abruptly whirred up from a rocky gorge well below Skye Fargo's position. He aimed his slitted gaze in that direction, mindful that he was conveniently skylined for any shooters hidden below.

"Spot any trouble, Mr. Fargo?" called out Owen Maitland from behind.

Maitland, a surveyor hired by the Northwestern Short Line Railroad, stood stooped over behind his Gunter's chain, sighting track bed for a new spur between Fort Laramie and the nearby settlement of Bear Creek.

"No Sioux or Cheyennes close by," Fargo replied, still studying the gorge below as he reined in beside a clear, sand-bottom creek. He threw off and then dropped the bridle so his Ovaro could drink. "But I spotted a she-grizz with cubs foraging not far from here. Keep your eyes peeled."

"I ain't scairt of no grizz," boasted Danny Ford, the green but likable kid who had been hired to hold the sticks for Maitland. "Mr. Fargo's got him a Henry rifle."

"You'd need a buffalo gun to drop a grizzly. Besides, I don't shoot anything or anybody if I can avoid it, Danny," Fargo replied absently. He was still watching that gorge below them while he stripped off his saddle and spread the sweat-soaked saddle blanket out to dry in the hot sun.

He was a tall, rangy, muscle-corded man with lake-blue eyes in a bearded and weather-tanned face. Several strings in the fringes of his buckskins were black with old blood. His eyes shifted to read the horizon, searching for dust puffs or reflections, looking for motion, not shapes. Then

1

his attention returned to the gorge, which he hadn't searched since early morning.

Maybe that was a mistake. . . .

Fargo definitely did not welcome the gut hunch he was feeling right now. He could find signs where most men saw only bare hardpan. Once, in a howling sandstorm, he had even tracked an unshod Comanche pony across New Mexico's blistering Staked Plain, a baked alkali hell drier than a year-old cow chip.

But the man some called the Trailsman had also learned to heed this "goose tickle" he felt now—a cold prickling on the back of his neck which only came just before all hell broke loose.

"Brother!" exclaimed Maitland, pausing to swipe at his sweaty brow with a handkerchief. "What I'd give right now to be drowning in an ocean of lemonade. That sun is hot as a branding iron."

Fargo, too, had been feeling the hot weight of the sun for several hours now. It was hard to believe there had been a thin powdering of frost on the grass when he rolled out of his blanket at dawn. Spring was a highly notional season in the Wyoming Territory.

He glimpsed a yellow coyote slinking off through the gorge below, not far from where the hen had flown up. Fargo relaxed a little, though he resolved to scout out that gorge again when the Ovaro had drunk and rested a little.

Fargo had been in the saddle since sunup, and his thighs and tailbone were sore. But even worse than the tiresome patrolling through rough terrain was his irritation with himself for accepting railroad money. He had been forced to find paying work for awhile—hell, he didn't have two nickels to rub together. He could hunt for his meals and sleep under the stars, but no amount of good trailcraft could provide ammunition, coffee, or a glass of beer. Only cold, hard cash.

But by now he knew the sickening pattern. Guns had gone from flintlock to cap and ball to the self-contained cartridge, and through most of that change the West had remained the same. However, the shining times were over.

Soon enough Maitland would be followed by track bed levelers, the pounding of spike mauls. First would come the early boomers, profiting quick and moving on. Then would come the cities with their foolish laws and rules so that a city dweller could never be truly free. "Cussed syphillization" as the old mountain men used to call it when a pristine wilderness began to settle up. The railroad plutocrats, the land-grabbers and strip miners had already washed in on a flood of eastern and foreign capital, a flood that was drowning out the strong-heart songs of the fur traders and Plains warriors.

Maitland had stopped work to build himself a smoke. He watched the Trailsman with friendly curiosity. The surveyor was a small, thin, middle-aged man wearing a boiled shirt, his sturdy canvas trousers tucked into calfskin boots. He had removed his high, glazed paper collar hours ago.

"Mr. Fargo," he remarked, "you do an excellent job of protecting me and Danny. But if you'll pardon my saying so, I get the distinct impression you'd rather be someplace else."

"This is fine country, and you and Danny are pleasant company," Fargo assured him honestly.

Fargo's pinto stallion lifted its nose from the creek, snorted, then stared toward the gorge below, sensitive nostrils quivering as they caught a scent.

Could be that coyote, Fargo told himself. But he felt the goose tickle again, like lice crawling against his scalp. He slipped the bridle back on, but the tired Ovaro resisted the bit.

"All right, old campaigner, a few more minutes," Fargo surrendered, grateful for the rest himself.

Maitland finished rolling his smoke, then expertly quirled the ends. He turned away from the wind to light it.

"If you can put up with this nursing job," he told Fargo, "the Santa Fe and Topeka Railroad is sending me down into the ass end of west Texas next. You're welcome to come along."

Fargo squatted on his heels and idly picked his teeth with a weed, his profile half in shadow under the slanted brim of his hat. Just west of this mostly flat tableland, the Laramie Mountains rose in ascending folds, the highest peaks still wearing ermine capes of snow. Due north, past the railroad tracks below and the rocky gorge beyond, the slopes were golden yellow with arrowroot blossoms. Here and there he spotted bright red splashes of the plant called Indian paintbrush.

Beautiful country, all right. But he glanced toward the east, where the short-grass prairie rolled on to the horizon, prime graze land. A stock tank was visible perhaps two miles distant. He had ridden past it earlier and seen a few mottled longhorns drinking—including some of the first seed bulls driven onto northern ranges from the cattle-rich *brasada* country of Texas.

Progress, some called it. Whatever its name, it dogged him like an afternoon shadow, always there when he glanced over his shoulder.

"Thanks for the offer," he finally replied. "But as soon as I'm not so light in the pockets, I'll be drifting on."

Maitland shrugged. "No harm in asking. I s'pose some fellows are just one-man outfits. Anyhow, won't be too long now and my rheumatism will have me all seized up in the hinges. Then I can retire to the liar's bench and brag how I tamed the West."

Danny had overheard them and now came running over. He was tall and gangly, with a wild shock of red hair, a snaggly-toothed grin and pants gone through at the knees.

"Can I go to Texas with you, Mr. Maitland?" he demanded in a welter of excitement. "I ain't got no ma or pa, so it's nobody's say-so if I go."

Fargo grinned at the kid. Danny spent most of his time in Bear Creek, mucking out stables and catching rats. Holding sticks for the railroad surveyor was the high point of his young life.

"What about Mr. Hupenbecker at the livery?" Maitland asked. "I thought he's your boss?"

"Aww, that's cowplop," Danny insisted. "Lookit Mr. Fargo, nobody tells him where he can work, do they?"

"Let it alone, Danny," Fargo advised the kid. "It's no big adventure to find yourself with the sun going low and no supper."

Or to constantly have gun sights notched on you, Fargo thought, deciding it was high time to scout out that gorge again.

This time his faithful Ovaro took the bit easily. Fargo was shaking burrs out of the saddle blanket when a steam whistle suddenly shrilled in the distance. The lonesome sound trailed off into silence except for the faint, rhythmic chuffing of the approaching locomotive, still out of sight from their position.

"The 2:20 from North Platte," Maitland announced.

"That's the orphan train!" Danny exclaimed. "And that pretty newspaper lady is with 'em!"

Even Fargo, who hadn't read a newspaper in weeks, knew about the much-ballyhooed orphan train that originated back east. Damndest thing he'd ever heard of. Evidently, Manhattan had become overrun with street urchins, and the publicity-hungry politician "Boss" Tweed had come up with a novel solution: Load the orphans aboard trains and send them out west, where settlers could look them over and pick the ones they wanted to come live with them.

Because there was still no unbroken link to railroads back east, the children had been transported, at times, by coach or flatboat. But the publicity-hungry railroads lost no opportunity to provide them free passage on any local short-lines, such as the one linking Fort Laramie to settlements due east. Fargo figured some of the unfortunate waifs would end up ill-used, turned into work horses. But others would find loving families. Almost anything was better than being abandoned to the mean city streets back east.

"What pretty lady might that be?" Fargo inquired as he centered his saddle.

"Gal named Kristen McKenna," Maitland replied. "Writes for the *New York Herald*, and I hear she's pretty as four aces. She's riding along to do stories on each kid that's picked by a family."

"Never heard of her," Fargo said, cinching his latigos.

Maitland's tone turned sly and teasing. "Then it sounds like she's about the *only* female that's escaped your notice. I heard about that little set-to last Saturday night at Lilly Ketchum's sporting house. How many of Sheriff Bolton's tinhorn deputies did you toss through the windows?"

Fargo feigned pure innocence. "All I remember rightly was all these starmen who kept running into my fists. Just clumsy, I expect."

"You'd best watch that bunch," Maitland suggested tactfully. "They're a secret ring, you ask me. A bunch of back-

5

scratching cousins. Bolton's one of those bribes or bullets sheriffs and he's related to most of his deputies *and* the judge. Those boys run Bear Creek like private property and tend to put the noose before the gavel. And it 'pears to me there's more and more rough fellows in this area eager to pin the no-good sign on you, Mr. Fargo. Especially the ones whose wives and sweethearts have heard of you."

Fargo stepped into a stirrup and pushed up and over. He tugged rein and wheeled right, heading down the face of the hill.

"Wives and sweethearts are safe with me," he called back over his shoulder. "Why toss your loop over branded stock when there's plenty of free-range mavericks?"

"You're telling me Lilly's sparkling doxies are *free*?"

"Damn, I wasn't s'posed to tell you paying men," Fargo shouted, and he heard Maitland laughing behind him.

Again the steam whistle shrilled, much closer now. The 2:20 from North Platte suddenly hove into view around the shoulder of Flint-Covered Mountain, the locomotive's diamond stack emitting huge, dark clouds of coal smoke. It was dramatically black against a vast, cloudless sky the pure blue of a gas flame.

The engine pulled a tender, four wooden coaches, and a caboose. Fargo glimpsed curious, pale young faces peering out of the windows. He booted the Ovaro up from a walk to a trot, figuring he could easily cross the tracks before the train reached him.

Less than a heartbeat later, things started happening ten ways a second.

With a huge, cracking boom, a section of track a hundred yards in front of the Trailsman suddenly exploded, ripped apart, and flew into the air. Fargo and his mount were showered in a descending cloud of dirt, rocks, and splintered ties.

The orphan train, moving along at thirty miles per hour, was only a few hundred yards from the blast area. The engineer could only throttle back, for the brakes were controlled by men stationed atop the passenger cars. Fargo, still wiping dirt from his eyes, watched the brakemen leap to their brake wheels and desperately start turning them.

Shots erupted from the rocky gorge north of the tracks. Fargo watched one of the brakemen, blood pluming from a chest hit, tumble dead to the ground beside the tracks. Another brakeman whipped a dragoon pistol out from under his duster and returned fire. He was hit a second later, dropping between two coaches. Fargo winced at the man's short, horrific scream before the train wheels crushed him.

When Fargo spotted masked men boiling out from the gorge, he whipped his Henry out of its saddle scabbard and levered a round into the chamber, throwing the weapon into his shoulder socket. Before he could even get a bead on one of them, however, withering gunfire erupted in his direction.

Like a sledgehammer blow, a round thwacked into his heavy leather gunbelt. Although the bullet failed to completely penetrate the thick leather, a white-hot pain grated in his left hip. Only his strong leg muscles kept him from being wiped out of the saddle.

Rounds filled the air around him, some passing so close they sounded like angry hornets. Fargo could see at least five men, all armed with rifles, and he knew they'd shoot him and the Ovaro to mattress stuffings if he foolishly kept charging across the open ground.

He rolled out of the saddle, tugging the reins as he fell to wheel the pinto around.

"Hee *yah*!" he shouted, slapping its glossy rump to send the well trained Ovaro back over the hill.

Fargo made himself so flat he felt like he was making love to the ground. A glance over his shoulder revealed Maitland and Danny, frozen with shock.

"Don't stand there with your thumbs up your sitters!" he shouted at them. "That's lead they're tossing at us! Cover down!"

He had no time to see if they followed his order, for just then the train hit the expanse of blown track. It had slowed considerably, but not enough to keep from jackknifing before it crashed at the bottom of the embankment, every car derailed except the caboose.

Two of the men in the gorge kept Fargo pinned while the rest went to work quickly and efficiently. At gunpoint they herded the dazed and shaken passengers, mostly kids, toward two buckboards waiting at the mouth of the gorge. When Fargo started to draw a bead, one of the men below

7

picked up a little girl in a calico frock and gray sunbonnet. He held his gun to her head, and a furious Fargo got the message. Feeling helpless and enraged, he lowered his Henry.

But the dry-gulchers didn't take just kids. Fargo watched one of them briefly struggling with a wheat blond beauty wearing a velvet-trimmed traveling suit. Even from his present position Fargo saw she had cheeks like fall apples and a bodice ready to rip from the strain of her full breasts.

Her lacquered straw hat, with its gay blue ribbon and bright ostrich feather, went sailing off into the wind when her captor suddenly slugged her, knocking her out. Anger and frustration simmering within, Fargo could only helplessly watch as the woman was tossed into one of the buckboards among crying and terrified children. He wasn't about to raise his rifle and get one of those kids killed.

The buckboards disappeared into the gorge. Fargo rolled to one side and shoved down his buckskin trousers to glance at his wound. No blood, just one hell of a bruise already coloring up. He pushed to his feet, whistling for the Ovaro.

Danny was the first to speak, his jaw falling open in pure astonishment. "Jiminy! Didja *see* that? Cripes, who was them men?"

"A litter of prairie rats, that's who," Fargo replied, catching hold of the Ovaro's bridle and stepping into leather. The stallion had whiffed blood from below and pranced nervously.

Maitland, pale as chalk, found his voice. "You going after them, Mr. Fargo?"

He shook his head. "Not now, or they'll be tossing dead kids off those buckboards. There's no other reason to grab those kids than a fat ransom from the railroad. It won't matter if their trail goes cold, a blind hog could track them. Right now there's dead and wounded below to tend to. C'mon."

But Maitland and Danny were still shocked and just stood there, staring in disbelief at the mangled train and dead bodies.

"Nerve up, you two!" he shouted in a tone they couldn't ignore. "This ain't some circus show, there's folks down there who need help."

8

Both men leaped into action as Fargo raced downhill toward the disaster scene. He paused only once, to lean down and pluck the woman's beribboned hat out of the grass.

It still bore a pleasant aroma of honeysuckle shampoo. He tucked it into one of his saddle panniers and promised himself he'd be returning it to that ample-bosomed beauty real soon.

2

New York Herald reporter Kristen McKenna sat on the board seat beside her captor, as stiff-spined as an angry preacher. Her lips were chapped with fear—fear for the crying and sobbing children and fear for her own safety. These coarse and raffish men were eyeing her as if they were all starving and she was the first meal they'd seen in weeks.

There had been forty children aboard when the orphan train pulled out from the terminal of the New York and Erie Line, amid great newspaper fanfare. A very capable matron had been sent along to help Kristen supervise the kids. But the matron had turned back at Ogallala, Nebraska, because by then most of the children had been placed with settlers. Kristen had insisted she could manage the dozen who still needed to find homes.

"Sir, this is madness!" she protested yet again to the driver of the lead buckboard, who also appeared to be the leader of the gang. "You can't get away with this . . . this outrage!"

Dakota Danford grinned at her as he poked a thin Mexican cigar between his teeth and thumb-scratched a lucifer to life, lighting his smoke with it. His lean, hard face was too mean to call handsome. Not once did his appraising gaze leave the comely woman. He had a jagged slash of tight-lipped mouth and deep-sunk eyes that delighted in shocking "quality women."

"Ain't nothin' on God's green earth gonna stop me, dumplin'," he assured her. "You and them little shirttail brats are gonna fetch a nice ransom: One hundred thousand dollars in gold double eagles, cash money over the counter."

"One hundred thousand! That's—why, it's a sheik's ransom!"

Danford's laugh was a harsh bark. "Call it sassafras, I don't care. Way I figure it, why keep going to the well for a cup at a time when you can just fill the bucket in one trip?"

"And just who is going to pay that kind of money? Certainly not the newspaper I work for."

"The only people who *got* that kind of money," he replied. "The railroad barons."

"Why are you so confident they will?"

"I can thank you for that, missy," he replied. "The railroads have been milking your stories on them kids. All that claptrap about how the locomotives represent a new life, new opportunities. They desert these little tadpoles now, the country will be howling for their hides."

"Judging from your tone, you must want that?" she pressed him, scared to push her luck but driven by reporter's curiosity.

His face twisted into a mask of bitter hatred. "I don't let *no* sons of bitches take what's mine. Not even them rich bastards back East who use them Philadelphia lawyers to get a man locked up."

"But what did they do to you that has you—?"

"Whack the cork, sugar britches. If I want your opinion, I'll beat it out of you with a rawhide strap. I can put another bruise on that pretty face of yours, so hobble your tongue."

"Miss McKenna?" called out seven-year-old Mattie from behind her. "Where are these men taking us? This ain't our new family, is it? I'm scared. They're mean men."

Kristen turned around and gave the little girl a quick, comforting hug. Wan and often poorly in health, sweet little Mattie was one of her favorites.

But in truth Kristen had come to love all of these kids. Ranging in age from six to fourteen, most had been abandoned in the notorious Five Points area, Manhattan's "cradle of gangs." They were now split up, six in this buckboard and six in the one following.

The man Danford had sent to scout the trail behind now loped up beside them astride a big seventeen-hand sorrel.

"Anybody on our spoor, Booth?" Danford asked him.

Booth Collins was an unkempt, rough-looking man with coarse-grained skin and a cauliflower ear from too much saloon brawling.

"Not a soul, boss," he replied, his eyes rushing over Kristen hungrily. She visibly shuddered as if he had touched her bare skin.

Danford noticed this and winked at Booth. Then he goaded Kristen with his grin. "Nobody's likely to be after us yet. That's on account them flabby bastards in town have read my note by now. And with my cousin Red in charge of the Bear Creek Vigilance Committee, won't nobody be lighting out after us—not right off, anyhow."

"That's mighty handy," Booth said, still undressing Kristen with his eyes. "Having your cousin as the acting sheriff hereabouts, I mean."

"Handy as a pocket in a shirt," Danford agreed. "How 'bout that bearded hombre riding the pinto stallion? No sign of him, neither?"

Collins snorted. "He's had his belly full of us, I'd wager. He's just some drifter the railroad hired on the cheap. Reece is pretty sure he tagged him with at least one bullet."

Danford nodded, reining in the team and turning to shout at the driver behind them. "Reece! Let's breathe the horses a spell."

The buckboard shifted on its springs when Danford lit down. He was a big, barrel-chested man, thick in the middle but more muscle than fat.

"Gotta shake the dew off my lily," he added, leering at Kristen. "Wanna come hold it for me, city princess?"

She flushed to the roots of her wheat blond hair while Dakota Danford and Booth Collins shared a laugh. As Danford headed toward a nearby clutch of rocks to do his business, Reece Jenkins wheeled the second buckboard up alongside the first. He had a string-bean build and wore a military cap with a havelock to protect the back of his neck from sun.

Jenkins and Collins studied the female reporter as if she were a rare museum exhibit.

"God a'mighty!" Collins exclaimed. "Look at the cat-heads on that wench! Maybe we best check her for a tit gun, Reece."

"Yeah boy," Jenkins chimed in, setting his brake handle and wrapping the reins around it. "*She* ain't no stable filly, is she? Just lookin' at her makes it a mite warm in my long-handles."

Despite her fear, Kristen bridled with anger.

"There are children present," she reminded them, a scalpel edge to her tone. "Please watch your language."

"Well, ain't *she* silky satin?" Collins jeered, dismounting and handing his reins to Jenkins. "You know what I'm thinking, Reece? I'd wager this little gal is wearing a pair of them frilly danties. Let's have a look-see."

He started to head around toward Kristen's side of the conveyance. Fear and disgust made her heart start hammering like fists on a drum. When Collins seized the hem of her skirt to lift it, she grabbed his hand and pushed it away. Kristen shuddered at the contact with his sweaty, filthy skin—it felt like handling raw bacon.

"Leave her alone, you filthy sage rat!"

The speaker was fourteen-year-old Terrance "Taffy" Mumford, the oldest of the dozen kids, who sat behind Kristen in the bed of the buckboard. Taffy was small but scrappy, a tough little Welsh kid whose father had been beaten to death by the highly feared Five Points gang known as the Plug Uglies. His mother died a year later from tuberculosis. Taffy was rescued from the East River docks by a church mission, but now was considered old enough to make his own way in Zeb Pike's Great American Desert, as many back east still called the West.

Collins stared at the kid from cold, smoke-colored eyes. "How'd you like to wear your ass for a hat, you little pee doodle?"

"Teach your grandmother to suck eggs, flap ear!"

Collins scowled darkly, for he was touchy on the subject of his misshapen ear. He ignored Kristen and stepped toward the back of the wagon.

"Well, Reece, looks like this scrawny pup thinks he's a full-growed dog," Collins muttered. "I'd say he needs to learn some respect for his betters."

"Mister, a pile of steaming horse turds is better than you. Smells better, too."

"Why, you mouthy little whelp! I'm gonna clean your plow, boy!"

Collins grabbed a handful of Taffy's shirt and started to haul him out of the buckboard.

"Booth! Never mind that." Danford emerged from the rocks, buttoning his fly.

"But, boss, this little mouthpiece just—"

"Never mind, I said. He'll get his, all in good time. This thing ain't even near played out."

The two men Danford had sent to ride their flanks— Nash Johnson and Heck Munro—now rode up to see what was going on.

"Lissenup, boys, while I got you all together," Danford called out. "For now I don't want any of these kids mistreated, that clear? Nor the woman either. You can look at her all you want, but for now nobody slices the loaf, hear me? We got us a powder keg on our hands here, and this thing's got to be did careful like. Somebody could be watching us right now. We turn this into a damned national crusade and our hash is cooked."

"It don't make sense nohow," Collins grumbled, staring at Kristen. "Peart-looking woman like her, and we can't even have a quick poke? Hell, I ain't never had a woman smells as good as her."

"All in good time, Booth, all in good time," Danford assured him as he climbed onto the buckboard seat again. "Once we got them gold shiners in our pockets, we'll *all* top her before we dust our hocks toward Mexico."

Danford kicked the brake off and flicked the reins to start the team.

"Let's break dust, boys," he called to the others. "Don't stop until we reach the yonder side of Middle Fork Creek."

Kristen had felt her blood ice at Danford's remark about "topping" her. In a way, she lamented, this was all somewhat her doing. With one immensely popular newspaper column, "What About the Least Among Us?," she had exposed the horrific plight of Manhattan's orphaned and abandoned kids. It had lit a reform fire under New Yorkers, not to mention the rest of the nation. And it was she who had inspired Manhattan's Fourth Ward leader, William "Boss" Tweed, to finally act.

Boss Tweed was notoriously crooked, but not heartless

where the poor were concerned. He lined his own pockets, but his Tammany Hall political machine had also built most of the city's charity hospitals and orphanages while the wealthy simply held their noses and complained. But the birthrate far outstripped any good intentions. So Boss Tweed met with Kristen and the *Herald* editor, starting the Frontier Kids program—one more source of the so-called orphan trains that brought youngsters to a new life in the American West.

Kristen had believed, at first, that mean prairies were better than mean city streets. So far she feared she was all wrong, and that it was too late to correct her terrible error.

"Please, Mr. Danford," she pleaded as the buckboard rattled and bounced over the uneven ground. "This is . . . why, it's just monstrous what you're doing! These children don't deserve this kind of treatment."

Danford shrugged his beefy shoulders. "Call it what you will, ink-slinger. All I know is, it sure's hell beats whipping beeves on the butt for thirty a month and found. The gods have pissed on me all my life. And when I finally snagged me a good job, the damned greedy railroad bosses ruin it for me over some damned stupid laws they claim I broke. So now it's *my* turn to ladle off the cream, and girl, I mean to slurp it."

Something had begun to gnaw at Kristen. Would Dakota Danford be talking so openly like this, in front of her, if he had any intention of letting her live? And if she didn't survive, what would happen to the children?

Danford, watching her from a slanted glance, saw Kristen suddenly go whey-faced. He gave another harsh bark of laughter.

"Finally figured it out, huh?" he teased her. "Pretty lady, your biggest mistake was when you forded the Mississippi River. Your 'Noo Yawk' airs don't cut no ice out here in sagebrush country. Won't be no heroes riding in to save your pretty skin, neither. Out here it's every fool for himself, and the devil take the hindmost."

Skye Fargo knew he'd be signing those kids' death warrants if he went charging off after them like a kill-crazy cavalry regiment. So instead he sent Danny into the nearby town of Bear Creek to report the incident and make sure a telegram was sent up the line to alert further rail traffic. In the meantime, Fargo and Owen Maitland did what they could for those injured in the derailing of the train.

Two brakemen had been murdered in cold blood, one so badly mangled by the train wheels that even the trail-hardened Fargo looked quickly away. Both the engineer and fireman suffered injuries, none life threatening. Fortunately, the orphan train was a special-order run, and no other passengers had been aboard.

"We've done what we can for now," Fargo told Maitland after rigging a splint on the engineer's broken leg. "You wait here, Owen, until help comes from town."

His well trained Ovaro had remained in the area without hobbles or tether, contentedly grazing on the slope above them. Fargo loosed a whistle and the stallion trotted down to join him.

"You ain't planning to go after those jaspers alone, are you?" Maitland demanded. "Hell, I counted at least five or six, all armed to the teeth."

Fargo stepped into a stirrup and swung aboard, sliding his Henry from its saddle scabbard to check the loads.

"Just a little scouting mission," he replied. "I don't want to play my hand until we know more about their demands. Right now I just want to ride their trail and see where they're headed. You recognize any of 'em?"

"I don't rile cool like you do, Mr. Fargo," Maitland replied sheepishly. "I got so goldang agitated I forgot to study their faces close. But one of them, the big, burly one built like a farmer's bull, was a dead ringer for Dakota Danford."

"That's a name I've heard in town. Who is he?"

"Red Bolton's cousin," Maitland explained, still eyeing the derailed locomotive and ruined stretch of railroad track bed. "Lives over in Hawk Springs, or use to. For several years he was the supervisor for the Wyoming division of the Overland Stage and Freighting Company. The job paid good, I hear. But when the Northwestern Short Line Railroad bought up the company, they cashiered him. Him and a bunch of the way station bosses who were in cahoots with him."

"Cashiered him? What for?"

"Evidently the man is crooked as cat turds. I heard he was pocketing money intended for the way stations—passengers are s'posed to get hot meals and decent liquor, but all they got on his watch was beans and creek water. And Overland had mail contracts, but little mail was getting through. Turned out the drivers, with Danford's encouragement, were tossing suitcases and valises, even mail sacks, into the mudholes during rainy weather so the stages wouldn't bog down and get off schedule. And plenty of passengers were being robbed when they spent the night at way stations in Danford's division."

"And you say it was the railroad that fired him," Fargo mused as he pressed the Ovaro lightly with his knees, starting toward the north. "See you back in town, Owen."

"You take care, Mr. Fargo. Dakota Danford is a fair hand with a gun, and he's so low-down mean and rotten he'd steal the coppers off a dead man's eyes. He's murdering scum and so's that bunch who side him. And I've heard rumors that a hired killer from Saint Louis has joined his bunch, a back-shooter named Booth Collins."

"I've had some experience with these unsavory types," Fargo assured him mildly as he rode off.

There were three large creeks located north of the blown railroad tracks, all about seven or eight miles apart and running parallel to each other: Bear Creek, which included a town of the same name, Middle Fork Creek, and Cheyenne Creek. He bore due north, following a trail so clear even a tenderfoot couldn't have missed it in the dark. Although Fargo knew little about the residents in this corner of southeastern Wyoming Territory, he knew the lay of the land well after two weeks of constant scouting. He wanted to confirm a gut hunch about where Danford—assuming it was Danford—and his gang were headed.

The natural beauty and peacefulness all around him seemed at odds with the ugly events of this day. The surrounding slopes were ablaze with wildflowers, the green grass so long and lush that it bent in the wind like furling waves. Far out on the flats to the east, he spotted a herd of pronghorn antelope. They were rabbit-hopping at great speed, white rumps flashing in the afternoon sun.

He was in no hurry to catch up with the buckboards, and

fully expected the kidnappers to send riders along their backtrail. Fortunately, deep washes scarred the landscape and provided good cover for his approach.

As he had guessed they would, the gang held to a due-north course, keeping the mountains on their left, the short-grass prairie to their right. By the time he reached the spot where they had forded Middle Fork Creek, Fargo was convinced he knew where they were headed—and the realization left a cold ball of ice in his stomach.

"They're headed for Devil's Catacombs, old friend," he remarked quietly to the Ovaro. "A lizard can't sneak up on 'em there."

The Devil's Catacombs were a series of connecting limestone caverns a short ride beyond Cheyenne Creek. Located in the high bluffs overlooking the creek, which was actually a river at this time of year, they offered an excellent defensive position. Anyone trying to approach from any direction could be seen from miles off. And the caverns themselves could not be reached except by a narrow bottleneck approach through massive walls of boulders. A few men with rifles and plenty of ammo could hold off a regiment.

In all the earlier excitement Fargo had forgotten to fill his canteen. Now his mouth felt as dry and stale as the last cracker in the barrel, and the last creek was well behind him. He popped a stone into his mouth and began sucking on it to slake his thirst.

There were still a few swallows of warm water sloshing around in his canteen. But it was his rule to never drink in the hot sun or he'd just sweat it out again. So he soaked his bandanna with the last of the water and used it to moisten the Ovaro's mouth, rinsing out the trail dust.

"Might as well head back to Bear Creek," he remarked to his mount as he forked leather again. "If that gang spots us, it could get ugly for them kids."

However, the Trailsman's hearing was as sharp as his legendary vision. And just then he heard it, riding on a wind current like a soaring hawk: the sound of a man's angry cursing. It came from just beyond the razorback ridge straight ahead.

Fargo quickly hobbled the Ovaro foreleg to rear behind

some screening timber, not wanting to take any chances despite the pinto's training. Then, sliding brass-framed army binoculars from a pannier and his Henry from its scabbard, he scuttled to the top of the ridge.

It was all laid out like a painting below him. Both buckboards had halted on the floor of a small canyon. The surrounding rock walls were banded with alternating layers of feldspar, quartz, and mica. The curses were coming from a big, ugly-mouthed man wearing a sidearm in a flap holster—Dakota Danford, Fargo guessed, recalling Maitland's description of a burly man "built like a farmer's bull."

He was roundly cursing the driver of the second buckboard. Fargo realized why when he raised the spyglasses and focused the lenses. A busted trace chain had immobilized the second conveyance.

Fargo shifted the glasses to the woman on the board seat beside Danford. Her opalescent skin was as smooth and flawless as a creamy lotion—except for a new bruise on her left cheek. For a moment she stared in Fargo's direction, and he saw that her eyes were the soft blue of forget-me-nots. Then he studied the kids in both buckboards—they looked scared spitless, especially the littlest ones, but otherwise unharmed.

He shifted the glasses back to the woman and had a few pleasant thoughts about what it might be like to learn the geography under her petticoats.

Reluctantly, he shifted his attention to several other riders milling around the buckboards. Fargo paid close attention to the mean-looking cur with the deformed ear. He rode a giant sorrel and sat an expensive, hand-tooled saddle with a high cantle and fancy silver trim. The holster of his short iron was tied low on his thigh, and the rear sight had been filed off so the weapon wouldn't snag coming out of the holster—sure signs of a professional gunman.

Fargo had never met Booth Collins, but suspected he was looking at him right now.

The last thing Fargo wanted, with a woman and kids in the way, was a shooting fray. But a man had to be ready to seize a chance when it presented itself. Using a long rock spur for cover, Fargo crept closer to the canyon floor.

Wind gusts blasted through the canyon, shrieking in the

nooks and crevasses—a mournful sound. However, when the wind abated, Fargo could hear snatches of Danford's shouted words.

". . . Reece, what makes you so damn hawg-stupid? You thick-skulled son of a bitch, I *told* you to replace that tug chain days ago! Now get it fixed quick and catch up to us. We'll take the rest of these whelps to Cheyenne Creek and make sure the ferry's waiting."

The others moved out, and Fargo permitted himself a little grin. Not only was opportunity knocking, it was leaning in to say howdy. True, this was only half the kids, but if he could snatch them back now, it would be a job well begun.

He crept closer, moving on the balls of his feet and letting wind noise cover his advance. The man called Reece had a percussion-action Sharps balanced across his thighs. But as he climbed down to work on the trace chain, he propped the Sharps against the front wheel of the buckboard.

"You damned brats pipe down," he growled at the kids, the smallest of whom were whimpering. "Or you'll get a taste of the cowhide."

His bullying words and tone sent angry bile spurting into Fargo's throat. Hell, with the exception of one boy who looked maybe ten or eleven, the rest of the poor little tykes in this buckboard were barely off ma's milk. Besides, now that he had a better look, Fargo recognized this man as the rifleman who had almost freed his soul back at the survey site.

But he patiently held his anger in check, watching while Reece used rawhide whangs to reinforce the broken chain. The moment he finished and reached for his rifle again, Fargo stepped out from behind the rock spur, Henry at the ready.

"Sorry to spoil your big time, mister," he called out in a tone that brooked no debate. "You touch that rifle and I'll be obliged to put an air shaft through you."

The driver whirled around, staring pop-eyed at the bearded, rangy stranger in buckskins. "What's your mix in this, mister?" he demanded.

"You ain't in charge here anymore, I am. So skip the questions. Now kick that rifle away from the buckboard."

Reece stubbornly shook his head. "You musta seen my partners just now ride out. You fire that smoke pole of your'n, the noise will fetch them down on you like ugly on a buzzard."

"That won't put breath back in *your* nostrils," Fargo warned him.

"I don't buffalo easy," Reece said belligerently, inching toward his rifle.

"Your last warning."

Reece was right on one score: Fargo had no intention of firing his weapon. But that's why he now held it in his left hand. Over the years he had gotten plenty of practice at raising his right foot and shucking his Arkansas Toothpick out of its boot sheath, all in one rapid, fluid movement quick as a finger snap.

And that's exactly how he did it now as Reece lunged for the Sharps. Fargo made one quick, hard, underhand flip, and a heartbeat later Reece was staring horrified at the blood spuming from his forearm, now pinned to the buckboard. He loosed a sharp yowl of pain even as he lunged for the rifle with his other hand. A moment later Fargo caught him solidly in the jaw with a roundhouse right, and Reece's knees folded under him. Fargo retrieved his knife and set to work tying his unconscious prisoner's wrists behind him.

"Way to go, mister!" cheered the oldest boy, leaping out of the buckboard. He was dressed in sailcloth pants and a thin corduroy coat. "You shoulda killed that horse's ass, he deserved it!"

Privately, Fargo agreed. The fool had gotten fair warning, backed by a loaded rifle. But he intended to make every last effort to minimize the ugliness these kids had to witness—the youngest ones, especially, knowing that they couldn't understand what was happening to them.

"You got a lot of mouth on you, colt," Fargo warned him. "Out west a man never cusses in front of females. Matter fact, you ain't even man-grown yet—you don't need to be cussing at all at your age."

"Why damn-it-to-hell not?"

Fargo swatted the kid on the butt and lifted him back into the buckboard.

"You little scamp, you lookin' to get us all plugged?

Them others could be sending a man back at any time. You hush up. We'll have time for proper introductions and chin-wag later. Right now we got to git."

Fargo, grunting at the effort, heaved his prisoner over the tailgate into the buckboard. Then he quickly tied off the wound with Reece's bandanna. He intended to make sure Peyton Norwood hired a couple of honest men to haul him to the stockade at Fort Laramie, at least for now. He quickly retrieved his Ovaro and tied him to the tailgate of the buckboard.

After a moment's thought, he also cut loose the goat gut filled with water tied to the tailgate. The rest of the gang would find it when they returned to check on the delay. There might not be much water near Devil's Catacombs, and Fargo had no intention of water-starving those remaining six kids and the woman reporter.

He quickly wheeled the buckboard around to the south and headed back toward Bear Creek, hoping he'd get enough of a start before the rest came back to check on their comrade and realized what had happened.

Fargo had wandered the West from the Rio Grande to the Tetons and points beyond. He'd seen crimes and acts of depravity even a dime novelist couldn't conjure up. But what he witnessed earlier today, the abduction of frightened, innocent children by murderous hard cases—it left a bad taste in his mouth. And it wouldn't wash out until justice was dispensed.

These children had seen enough misery in their young lives, they didn't deserve this. And come hell or high water, he vowed, he would rescue the rest of those kids, or die trying.

3

Bear Creek was a crossroads settlement that began as a stage stop. The place was still so new that some of the dwellings were little more than shanties and hutches covered with wagon canvas.

Nonetheless, the wagon-rutted main street was currently boiling with activity. News of the bold kidnapping earlier that day had lured many of the outlying settlers and even some folks from Fort Laramie and beyond. And although Bear Creek had only one saloon, a crude canvas-and-clapboard structure, a number of Temperance women were taking advantage of the crowds to march out front of it. They carried signs that read THIS IS THE GATE TO HELL and GOD'S LAST NAME ISN'T DAMNIT!

It was into the midst of this frontier bedlam that Skye Fargo drove the buckboard filled with six rescued kids and a prisoner. A hush came over the throng, many staring at the buckskin-clad, weather-tanned driver—a tall man whose shadow seemed even longer in the waning sun. Most had heard he was in the area, but few had ever seen him before.

"It's the Trailsman!" somebody sang out. "And he's saved some of the kids!"

A cheer erupted, and Fargo patiently endured the backslapping, glad-handing, and congratulations of well-wishers. He knew there was also hostility and suspicion in the eyes and minds of some who were watching him. A man who kept to himself was always suspect—few townspeople could abide a bunch-quitter like Skye Fargo.

And one of them, self-appointed Sheriff Red Bolton,

was watching him from the shadow of the jailhouse, his face hard as granite behind a longhorn mustache.

Fargo's prisoner had come to by now and was sitting with his knees drawn up under his chin, his face a sullen deadpan.

"Why, that's Reece Jenkins!" a voice shouted from the throng. "He use to manage a way station for Overland in Dakota Danford's division."

Fargo paid close attention when Bolton and Jenkins exchanged a long look—Bolton seemed to nod almost imperceptibly.

Spotting the scared and exhausted children, the stern-faced Temperance biddies immediately tossed aside their signs and ran over to mother the children.

A long-faced and narrow-shouldered man with bushy gray muttonchops shouldered his way through the crowd toward Fargo. Many folks stepped respectfully aside, for the man was well turned out in a shirt of finespun linen, an octagonal tie, fancy oxblood boots, and a wool topcoat.

"Congratulations, Fargo!" Peyton Norwood greeted him, giving him a hearty grip. "I knew you had starch, that's why I hired you to protect Owen Maitland. Any word on Miss McKenna and the rest of the kids?"

Fargo could barely hear the railroad official above the noise of the clamoring crowd. He climbed down off the buckboard, slapping the dust from his hat. Again his gaze shifted toward Red Bolton's stern-featured face. The man hardly appears glad to see these young'uns, Fargo mused.

"There's some word, Mr. Norwood," Fargo replied. "They're all still alive. But this isn't the time or place to report. First I need to tend to my horse."

"Of course, of course."

Fargo hooked a thumb toward Jenkins. "He's one of the kidnappers. Is there someplace to keep him under guard besides the town jail?"

Norwood looked startled. "Well . . . there's the freight office. I have two railroad guards there."

Fargo nodded. "I know 'em both, good men. Can you arrange to have them take the prisoner to Fort Laramie?

Right now I'm not so sure Bear Creek will hold him long."

Fargo said this loud enough for Red Bolton to overhear. The self-appointed lawman turned and faded into the shadows of the alley.

Norwood, however, quickly nodded agreement. He seemed a little too eager to curry favor. He inclined his head in the direction of a low building made from cottonwood logs and mud, the new railroad office at the western outskirts of town. "My office then, Mr. Fargo? Say, in a half hour? Sheriff Bolton will be present, too. Naturally he's champing at the bit, eager to get after these scoundrels."

"Naturally," Fargo repeated in a flat tone as he untied the Ovaro from the back of the buckboard. "See you in a bit."

The kids, practically smothering in affection and concern, had already been rushed off to various homes for baths and hot meals.

Leading his Ovaro by the bridle reins, Fargo headed toward the livery stable down the street. Slappy Hupenbecker, the grizzled old former trapper now turned hostler, was smashing flies with a quirt when Fargo led his horse through the wide side doors.

"By Godfrey, it's Skye Fargo!" Slappy greeted him. "A bullet ain't found his brainpan yet! Let's pull a cork to the old ways, hoss."

Young Danny Ford was at work at a nearby bench, pounding caulks into old horseshoes, when the Trailsman arrived. The kid tossed aside his hammer and flashed Fargo a snaggly-toothed grin.

"Mr. Fargo! Didja find the kids, huh? Didja blow holes in them polecats what wrecked the tra—?"

"Danny, take a breath," Fargo cut him off. "Half the kids are safe. And no, I didn't shoot anybody. But one of those polecats is lucky he ain't walking with his ancestors right now."

Danny's boy-howdy enthusiasm coaxed a grin out of Fargo. He accepted a jug of cheap 40-rod whiskey from Slappy and knocked back a slug, feeling it burn in a straight line to his gut.

"Slappy, that coffin varnish you drink would raise blood blisters on leather," Fargo joked as he stripped off the Ovaro's saddle and tossed it onto a rack in the tack room. He could have let Danny do it, but Fargo liked to inspect his stallion close for saddle galls.

Slappy, wearing old stovepipe trousers gone shiny in the knees, took a long pull from the jug, then wiped his mouth on his sleeve and winked at Fargo.

"It's medicine, Skye, not sippin' whiskey. My insides is all shifted ever which-way from my bronc-bustin' days. I take a nip now and agin for the pain, is all. But, say! Hell's a-poppin' hereabouts, young feller. Folks is all wound up to a fare-thee-well over these missing youngsters and that pretty gal reporter with the big knock—"

Slappy caught himself just in time, remembering Danny.

"With the big reputation," he amended. "And that surveyor fellow, Owen Maitland, claims Dakota Danford and his bunch are behind it. You watch that bastard, Skye, watch him like a cat on a rat. Danford ain't just mule mean—I don't think all his biscuits are done, if you take my drift? That man hoards grudges the way misers hoard gold. And he's got him a powerful grudge agin' the railroads."

Fargo had rubbed down the Ovaro and now was currying the dried sweat off its flanks. " 'Preciate the warning, old timer. What can you tell me about his cousin, Red Bolton?"

"That blowhard? The gum'ment ain't sent us no U.S. marshals out this way yet, so Bolton has set hisself and his vigilance committee up as the law in this area. He's alla time a-puffin' and a-blowin', the on'ry sumbitch. Swaggers it around actin' like he's some pumpkins. Likes to throw parties, too—necktie parties. He's left plenty of men dancing on air because we can't hardly get no circuit judges to ride out this way and stop the lynchings."

Fargo nodded, letting all this information settle in. "Tell me straight, Slappy—is this so-called sheriff *close* cousins with Danford? Close enough to be in cahoots with him?"

The old hostler gave Fargo a puzzle-headed grin. "Now as to that question—it's a real stumper. I wouldn't 'zacly say they're tight as ticks, no. But just like his cousin, Red Bolton is mean—meaner than Satan with a sunburn. He ain't quite right in his upper story, neither. You watch him close. He's a kill-fighter—never just whips a man. Always got to leave him dead. Claims he won't humble a man, then let him live to seek revenge."

"Bolton sounds like a hard twist, all right," Fargo remarked.

"Word is," Danny cut in excitedly, "that railroad fellow, Mr. Norwood, is gonna see can he hire you to track down Danford's gang. Can I be your pard, Mr. Fargo, huh? Can I ride with you? Mr. Maitland won't need me to hold the sticks for him on account there won't be no more surveying till all them kids is saved and the railroad tracks is fixed."

"Air ye daft, lad?" Slappy demanded. "Hell, you're hardly out of three-cornered britches, and you expect to brace the likes of Danford and his killers? Only time that bunch looks at a fella is when they're measuring him for a casket."

"Slappy's right," Fargo said. "You got some growth to get yet, son."

"Aww, that ain't fair, I—"

"Clean your ears or cut your hair," Slappy cut in. "Mr. Fargo says no. Besides, I'm gettin' a mite long in the tooth, Danny boy. Why go get yourself kilt when you'll be in charge of the livery soon enough?"

"I don't care to own it," Danny said stubbornly. "You work this place from get up to go to bed, and you're still poor as Job's turkey. You always say so yourself."

Danny turned pleading eyes on Fargo. "Them kids is just like me, Mr. Fargo, no ma nor pa. I wanna help 'em."

Some deep yearning in the kid's manner touched Fargo. "Well . . . we'll see. Are you a good horse-backer, Danny?"

The kid's face lit up like a Roman candle. "You bet your bucket I am! You just get me a gun, and—"

Fargo raised a hand to shush him.

"Now look, Danny, we ain't joined at the hip. Ease off on this talk about guns. I said *maybe* you can help out, and by that I mean I might need a messenger rider.

27

We'll talk more later after I parley with Norwood. Right now you've got my horse to finish taking care of."

He pointed at a tender swelling on the Ovaro's right flank. "See there? I girthed him too tight for the terrain we covered. Smear plenty of gall salve on that. Then I want you to grain him good, oats and corn. And don't stall him tonight unless it rains, he ain't used to being cooped up. Turn him out into the paddock."

"Yessir! I'll treat him like the great war horse he is."

"Another thing, Danny—graze may get scarce where I'm headed. Stuff the panniers good with plenty of oats."

"Skye!" Slappy called out as the Trailsman headed outside. "You watch that Norwood close too. Them big railroad nabobs are slicker than snot on a doorknob. And that bunch of Red Bolton's ain't nothin' but yellow-bellied eggsuckers. The way things stand around this town, you might be walkin' right into a stacked deck."

Fargo still had ten minutes or so to kill before his meeting with Norwood and Bolton. What he really needed to do was cut the wolf loose for a day or so. But a quick beer, to cut the bad taste of Slappy's wagon-yard whiskey, would have to do for now.

The Last Alibi saloon was a bit less rustic on the inside than its squalid exterior suggested. Fargo's boot heels drummed on a solid plank floor sprinkled with sawdust. A blue pall of tobacco smoke filled the place, so thick it hung from the ceiling like old sacking. There were a few card tables with green-baize tops, and several dime-a-dance girls wearing feather boas gave him lingering glances.

As did a few rough and unshaven men scattered about the barroom—men wearing the tin stars of the Bear Creek Vigilance Committee. But their cold-steel stares were much less promising and inviting than those of the females.

Fargo bellied up to the raw-plank bar, carefully placing his elbows to avoid the slops.

"Beer," he told the big, soft-bellied barkeep. "And don't draw it too nappy."

"On the house," the bar dog replied, plunking down a mug in front of Fargo. "That was some piece of work you done, fetching them six kids back safe. I got a few pups on the rug myself, Mr. Fargo."

" 'Preciate the drink and the kind words, friend."

Fargo quaffed half the brew in one deep swallow. In the bar mirror, he watched one of the men wearing a tin star scrape back his chair and head toward the bar.

"Say, mister?" the stranger said, crowding next to Fargo at the bar. "I recognize you. Wasn't you a contract scout for the army down in Navajo country?"

"Several times, matter of fact."

"Yeah? And I'm told you can track a bug across bare rock."

"Oh, I get lucky now and again," Fargo replied in his mild way, wondering where this trail was headed.

"Luck ain't always predictable. Just a friendly tip, mister. Word has it the railroad means to hire you instead of using local law to go after these kids and the woman. But around here, the nail that sticks up gets hammered down."

Fargo finished his beer and sleeved foam off his whiskers. "That's mighty tall talk, coming from a man who says he's just being friendly."

"No, it ain't tall talk. Rumor has it there's an hombre named Booth Collins that's among this bunch of kidnappers. Mister, Booth Collins can light matches with a pistol at thirty feet. I seen him do it."

Fargo pushed away from the bar and squared off in front of the speaker, balanced on his heels for trouble. He was now within an ace of cold-cocking Bolton's toady. Then he realized: That's probably exactly what Bolton and his bunch wanted—an excuse to toss Skye Fargo in the calaboose. He could hardly go after Cousin Danford while cooling his heels in a jail cell.

"Well, matches don't shoot back, do they?" Fargo replied. "Thanks for the drink, Bottles," he called out to the barkeep before he shouldered past the tinhorn deputy and headed out into the street again.

Fargo thumped along the boardwalk until he reached the office of the Northwestern Short Line. The moment he opened the street door, a pale clerk in sleeve garters and green eye shades escorted him into Norwood's private office.

Norwood was pacing nervously in front of his desk. Red Bolton had sprawled in a cowhide chair, his feet propped up on a cold stove with nickel trimmings. He was casually cleaning his fingernails with a horseshoe nail.

"Mr. Fargo!" Norwood greeted him, hurrying to shake his hand for the second time that day. "We've just received a telegraph message from the regional office in Omaha. They're overjoyed at your rescue of half the children. Oh, by the way—I take it you've met Sheriff Bolton?"

Fargo's lake-blue gaze shifted toward Bolton. "We've seen each other around," he replied. "Though I noticed him and his . . . deputies were mighty scarce today during and after the attack on that train."

Bolton's feet hit the floor with a loud thump as he sat up straighter, mud-colored eyes staring hard at the Trailsman. Evidently, Red Bolton had a personality as dour as his face.

"You're taking the long way around the barn, Fargo," he growled. "If you're accusing me of something, spit it out plain."

"All right, I will. I saw you watching when I brought those kids in. And your face looked like somebody just kicked your dog. As for your 'men'—they're all over in the saloon sitting on their asses. I don't think you give a tinker's damn what happens to them kids and the reporter. Is *that* too rich for your belly?"

Red Bolton was not used to having his authority challenged. His neck swelled and his face turned brick red.

"That's a bald-faced lie!" he retorted hotly. "Don't lay the blame at my door, Fargo. Mr. Norwood here asked me to hold back. It's that damned newspaper woman's fault. And where do you come off arresting Reece Jenkins on your own authority? I—"

"Now, gentlemen," Norwood interceded, pouring oil on the waters. "Lower the hammer, both of you. We're all on the same side here. The sheriff is right, Mr. Fargo, I did request that he take no action."

Norwood pointed toward a big wall map behind his desk. It depicted America west of the Mississippi River.

"Mr. Fargo, ideally we would call on the U.S. Army

30

to handle this thing. But no doubt you've heard the rumors of a great civil war brewing back east. Soldiers are being called back in huge numbers. Right now they're stretched very thin—only about fifteen hundred left to cover the entire American frontier. Hell, that's like trying to hold the ocean back with a broom."

Fargo nodded. "I'll grant all that. It still doesn't explain why you've held back from sending out a citizens' posse."

"Perhaps this will help explain it," Norwood replied, sliding a folded sheet of paper from his coat pocket and handing it to Fargo. "It was pushed under our door sometime earlier today."

Fargo read the brief printed message:

IF YOU HOPE TO GET THE WOMAN AND KIDS BACK ALIVE, IT WILL COST YOU $100,000 IN GOLD DOUBLE EAGLES. SEND *ONE MAN ONLY* TO BRING IT TO DEVIL'S CATACOMBS. WE DON'T PLAN TO HURT ANY OF THE CAPTIVES. BUT IF YOU PUSH US TO IT, THEY'LL ALL BE SLAUGHTERED LIKE HOGS.

Fargo stared at Norwood. "That's a sight of money. The railroad actually means to pay it?"

Norwood shrugged helplessly. "Our goose was cooked when all the big newspapers recently formed this damned Associated Press for sharing telegraphic dispatches. Now, every time there's a problem involving the railroads, it gets splashed all over the country."

"Damn shame you can't hide your dirty linen," Fargo remarked.

Norwood ignored that. "The lack of security aboard trains is a hair-trigger topic these days. And thanks to Miss McKenna's talent as a writer, the whole nation—hell, much of Europe, even—is following the fate of these waifs. We've decided to pay, Mr. Fargo, and we need a man like you to deliver the ransom."

Something occurred to Fargo, and he recalled that deputy's attempt to goad him into violence in the barroom. Now it became clearer why they wanted him out of the way.

"You mean to tell me," Fargo said, "that Bolton here

31

hasn't offered to do it? Everybody claims it's his cousin behind all this. Why not keep it in the family?"

"He did indeed offer, most strenuously," Norwood replied, confirming Fargo's hunch. "But the head office is in charge of this . . . delicate matter, and they don't want it done slapdash, no offense, Red. They demand I get the best man I can get."

Bolton frowned so deeply his eyebrows touched over his nose. "So you trust this damn drifter with all that money?"

"Mr. Fargo just 'drifted' into town, Red, with half the kids."

"Yeah, but—"

"Stick your 'buts' back in your pocket, Bolton," Fargo cut him off impatiently. "There ain't no time for pissing fights over who's the big he-dog hereabouts. It's time to quit jaw-boning and get them kids and the woman back."

Norwood's face brightened. "So you'll do it?"

Fargo nodded. "I'll ride out at first light. Where's the gold?"

"Under guard at the Wells Fargo office. You'll need a packhorse to haul it—it weighs over a hundred pounds."

Fargo looked at Bolton. "Sounds too easy, to me. I expect there'll be a double cross of some kind."

"That's why I better ride with you," Bolton said.

Fargo shook his head. "I work alone."

"Has your brain come unhinged? They—"

"Gentlemen, please!" Norwood pleaded. "I have enough on my plate as it is. The Northwestern Short Line has got that blown railbed to repair, and a derailed train to deal with. I don't need this clash of stags."

"I work alone," Fargo repeated, "or Mr. Norwood can get another man for the job."

"Mr. Fargo is calling the shots, Red," Norwood insisted. "His reputation has preceded him, and he's earned the right to dictate terms."

"Much obliged," Fargo said, turning toward the door. But he felt Bolton's hate-filled stare on his back, and Fargo knew he had just signed on for yet another suicide mission.

4

"C'mon, sugar tits," Booth Collins slurred drunkenly, "let's me and you pitch a little hay, hanh?"

Kristen, busy cooking bacon and panbread in an iron skillet, pretended to ignore the filthy hyena. He leered at her across a fire pit, dug near the cave entrance so smoke would clear out.

Collins, an ugly man who became even uglier when drunk, took another swig from his bottle of rye.

"Yessir, you got a damn *fine* set of puffy loaves, cotton-tail," Collins mumbled, staggering toward her. "I mean to have me a little peek at them darlin' dugs. And I'm still waitin' to see them frilly dainties."

Adroitly, Kristen ducked out of his reach, keeping the fire pit between herself and Collins.

"You animal!" she hurled at him. "Have you *no* shame? Can't you see the children are all watching and listening?"

The six children who had not been rescued yesterday now huddled at the rear of the spacious cavern. Some still lay on the crude shakedowns of filthy straw that served as beds. This was one of the largest of the dozens of caves that made up the Devil's Catacombs. They pockmarked the steep, wooded bluffs overlooking the spring-swollen Cheyenne Creek. Some were hardly more than snake dens and hidey-holes barely large enough for hibernating bears. A few others were roomy caverns like this one.

This cavern had been a robber's roost since the first large westward migrations began in the 1840s, and by now it had even acquired a few comforts, probably discarded by migrating settlers with overloaded wagons. There were a few three-legged stools scattered about, and a crude table made by nailing some planks to a pair of trestles. There was even a big rug braided from rags, which covered much of the cold dirt floor of the cave.

"*Let* the little whelps watch us," Booth replied, lunging at Kristen again. "You think farm kids don't never see nature take her course?"

This time Booth, trailing a strong reek of whiskey, managed to grab her before Kristen could duck. He caught her from behind and cupped his hands on the firm swell of her bodice.

"Let me *go*, you disgusting pig!"

"Hot damn, you *are* a firebrand!" he slurred drunkenly, trying to rip open the stays on her bodice.

"Leave her be, you ignorant peckerwood!" shouted Taffy Mumford, the oldest of the captive children. He rushed forward and tried to tackle Collins. With an angry growl, Collins backhanded the kid hard, sending him sprawling.

But at least Taffy's bravery had freed Kristen from Collins's odious grip. As he advanced on Taffy, preparing to beat the kid senseless, Kristen seized the skillet with its sizzling grease.

"You touch him again," she threatened, "and I'll make the rest of your face look like your ear!"

"Why, you saucy little she-devil," Collins said, sliding the riding thong off the hammer of his six-shooter and shucking it out of the holster. "I'm done askin' polite. Now, you peel off them clothes—including your dainties."

"Booth! Holster that shooter, you damned fool!"

The speaker was Dakota Danford, who had just stepped into the cave accompanied by Nash Johnson and Heck Munro.

"Unpucker your asshole," Booth said defiantly, though he did holster his gun. "That big-city slut has got a tart mouth on her."

"T'hell with that," Danford snapped. "I told you yesterday—*none* of the captives gets hurt until them gold shiners are safe in our hands. Matter fact—"

Danford aimed his deep-set, flint-eyed gaze at Kristen. "Soon's you feed them brats, woman, I want all of yous outside soaking up that nice early morning sunshine, hear me? Just in case we got some sharpshooters down there by the creek notching their sights on this cave."

Booth scowled. "I thought you said there wouldn't be nobody but your cousin Red coming this way, bringing us the gold?"

"Sober up, you puddin' head," Danford snapped. "Do you think it was my cousin what got the jump on Reece yesterday and rescued them other kids? It had to be that bearded stranger we spotted when we blew up the tracks."

"Who in the hell *is* he?" chimed in Nash Johnson, who held a Volcanic lever-action repeating rifle tucked under his arm. He had small, dull eyes like a turtle. But Nash was as deadly with a rifle as Booth Collins was with a short gun.

"Damned if I know," Danford replied. "When we first seen him scouting awhile back, I just figgered he was some bag-line bum fired from one of the ranches hereabouts. But he sure's hell ain't no dirt-scratcher or cow nurse. Not if he got the drop on Reece. Reece ain't no milk liver, yet it 'pears this stranger bested him."

"So what?" Collins said, still staring at Kristen as she dished up the kids' breakfast into wooden bowls. "With Reece dealt out, that's one less man we gotta split the swag with."

"That ain't the point, you drunken sot. That jasper on the pinto stallion works for the railroad, and it just might be that *he's* the one they'll send riding up with the gold, not my cousin. That means—"

Danford fell silent, realizing that Kristen had one ear cocked toward what he was saying.

"You, ink-slinger," he snapped. "Now you got them vittles cooked, you and them kids go sit outside and eat."

Glad to obey, Kristen herded the kids out into the warm morning sunshine.

"Where *you* going?" Danford demanded when Booth started to follow them outside.

"To keep an eye on the woman. You been too free about lettin' her wander around out—"

"Damnit, Booth, think with your brain, not your cod! Where the hell is she gonna go with six kids in tow? Just sprout wings and *fly* off this bluff? And who wet nurses them brats if she leaves them to run off? We *want* them moving around up here just in case we're being watched."

Dakota paused to pull the watch out of his fob pocket, thumbing back the cover to read the time.

"The day's still a pup," he said. "If Red, or whoever's coming with the gold, waited until after sunup, it'll still be hours before he gets here. Nash?"

"Yo!"

"There's only one trail leads up to here. You're so sharp with a rifle you can shoot the eyes out of a turkey buzzard at two hunnert yards. Just a little ways down the trail from here there's a cutbank behind a rock spine. You can see clear into next week from there. If it's Cousin Red riding in, you'll know it from his big claybank gelding and that gray hat he always wears, the one with the rattlesnake band on the crown."

Danford paused. For a moment, to emphasize his next point, he rested his hand on his Smith & Wesson magazine pistol in its flap holster.

"If it's anybody else but Red," he continued, "that means it's a double cross by them railroad bastards. Anybody but Red, and I want him dead, Nash, dead as last Christmas. Y'unnerstan'? Then we'll grab the gold and slip out by the secret tunnel, then light a shuck for Old Mexico."

Now Danford turned his gaze on Booth. "And if they come at us with *more* than one rider, some kind of posse, you'll kill one of those brats and throw it off the bluff. Or as many as it takes to stop 'em. You got the belly for that?"

Collins snorted. "Does a whore have wrinkled bed sheets? Hell, I shot an old man once for snoring too loud. Don't worry 'bout old Booth Collins. I'd kiss the devil's ass in hell for the gold we stand to make."

Dakota nodded, his eyes puckering with satisfaction. "*Now* you're whistling. Because the plain truth is, we are gonna toss them brats off the bluffs. Just as soon as we got that gold. You think I'm lettin' them chicken-gutted railroad bosses get off the hook so easy after the way they done us? Truth is, most folks hate the railroad barons. So once it makes the newspapers, and all of us have hightailed it to Mex, the blood of them dead kids will be on railroad hands. We might even bankrupt the Northwestern Short Line while we are living high on the hog and toppin' them pretty sen-yer-eeters."

"Speaking of that," Heck Munro spoke up, "we ain't

goin' to waste that McKenna gal, are we? That's a fine piece of woman flesh."

"One quick poke apiece," Dakota promised. "Soon's we got the gold. And after we've all had a whack at her, she goes over the bluff, too."

In all her twenty-six years of life, Kristen McKenna had never been this frightened. Or had so much to worry about with no one to help her.

Her heart broke anew as she watched the children seated around her in a semicircle, listlessly eating their breakfast. She had been elated when she first realized, eavesdropping on her captors late yesterday, that six of the kids had somehow been saved. Hope sprang up within her only to be dashed by the last leg of their journey to this isolated fortress.

They had been forced to leave the buckboard at the creek, riding up the steep, narrow trail on a string of horses now tethered in the woods atop the bluffs. From up here a sentry could see anything—even a prairie dog—from miles off. And she was beginning to suspect that Danford, a man brimming with personal hatred for the railroads, had no intention of trading captives for money.

She would be killed, Kristen suspected, and worse—she would be "outraged" by these stinking men, the polite term for rape. And a fresh tumult of misery swept through her as she glanced around at all the children. They too would die, innocent pawns plucked from the streets of Manhattan to be sacrificed in a sick man's cruel game of greed and revenge.

Besides tough-talking Taffy, the oldest, and seven-year-old Mattie, her secret favorite, there was Mattie's big sister Sarah, who was twelve; there was eleven-year-old Liam and his ten-year-old friend Dominic, who insisted on being called Nick because it sounded more American. Nick, once run over by a dray wagon on Fulton Street, was very defensive about his pronounced limp.

And most worrisome of all, to Kristen: six-year-old Virginia "Ginny" Andrews, a shy, abused child who had literally clammed up since this nightmare ordeal began yesterday. Seldom talkative anyway, she had now completely withdrawn into herself.

Kristen recalled a line from her column "What About the Least Among Us?": *A child's problems are small, certainly. But then, so is the child.* Well, they certainly had big problems now.

"Eat your breakfast, Ginny," she said in a gentle tone. But Ginny only pushed her bowl toward Taffy so he could eat it.

This was too much for Kristen, who now felt tears stinging her eyes and throat. A good cry was coming on. Yet, she dare not break down in front of the children, for she was their only source of strength.

Fortunately, Danford had been tolerant on one point: Since escape was no threat, she and the children were allowed to freely come and go to make "necessary trips" and to bathe. In a pine-sheltered hollow beyond the cave entrance, there was a little pond fed by a quiet rill. While there were only six of them, Kristen was amazed at how many "necessary" times there were when you were under twelve.

Fargo had got an early start that morning and pushed the Ovaro and packhorse hard, wanting to reach Cheyenne Creek before Danford's gang would be expecting anyone. Now he was hidden in a clump of hawthorn bushes and juniper trees along the south bank of the rushing creek, carefully getting the lay of the land up on the bluffs.

He scanned the bluffs with his binoculars, immediately spotting the six kids, sitting near the entrance to one of the biggest caves. He also saw rifle-toting men coming and going, obviously keeping watch on the flats below. Unfortunately, a big jumble of rocks kept him from spotting their exact sentry positions near the head of the steep trail.

Staying low, Fargo backed into the screening timber where he had ground-hitched both horses. His ride, earlier that morning, had proved uneventful. He had passed no one on the trail except an early-rising old farmer hauling crated chickens. And by now he knew the gang had discovered the loss of Reece Jenkins and six of their hostages.

So Fargo fully expected trouble, and plenty of it. The way he figured things, Dakota Danford and his bunch knew damn well they were gone beavers if they were ever caught—whether or not they turned over those captives as promised. After all, they had murdered train crewmen in cold blood, extorted money, and sabotaged a train. They would not face a jury. It would be a virtual hemp committee, fitting all of them for a richly deserved rope.

And given Danford's apparent grudge against the railroads, killing those captives was probably a key part of his plan. Nonetheless, Fargo meant to follow instructions—at least, at first. He had to for the children's sake. But under no circumstances was he surrendering that gold until all those captives were free.

Anticipating trouble, Fargo had parleyed the night before with young Danny Ford and the surveyor, Owen Maitland. Owen, smart and well-liked around town, promised to keep a close eye on Red Bolton and his men. Danny was to serve as daily message rider between Owen and Fargo. But Fargo gave the green-antlered kid strict orders not to ride farther north than Middle Ford Creek, the one located midway between this spot and Bear Creek. Any messages would be left in a lightning-split cedar tree Fargo had described to him.

Fargo glanced at the sky as he untethered both horses: almost eight a.m., by the sun. Time to ride into the belly of the beast. . . .

He mounted the Ovaro and wrapped the packhorse's leadline around his saddle horn—it was a big gray gelding draped in gold-laden packs. Fargo held the Ovaro to a trot as they headed toward the nearby gravel-bar ford. Spring snowmelt from the nearby mountains had swollen the big creek to the top of its grassy banks, and the current was fast.

He spotted the abandoned buckboard well before he reached the ford. It sat on the north bank, ferried across by a rope-guided raft now tied to a tree on the south bank. Either they had killed the ferry operator or he wasn't an early riser, for there was no sign of him.

Knowing he was now in full view of any sentries up on the bluffs, Fargo swung down and untied the ferry, leading both horses onto it. The Ovaro could easily have swum this crossing, but the gold-laden packhorse might have trouble. Fargo heaved on the guide rope, pulling them slowly across the brawling, frothing water. Sweat eased out from under his hat band, for Fargo realized he would soon be within rifle range and as vulnerable a target as a duck sitting on a fence.

He lingered a bit on the opposite bank and squatted on his heels to read the sign. There were many animal tracks here because a gravel bar provided a natural ford. Most of the hoof prints were unshod, either made by Indian ponies or the many half-wild mustangs in this area. But he counted at least a half-dozen sets of iron-shod hooves. Clearly the kids and Kristen McKenna had been hauled up the steep trail riding double on the horses of their captors.

He used the toe of his boot to break open some fresh horse droppings: grain droppings, not grass. His enemies were evidently well provisioned for a long siege, if the need arose.

"Well, let's get this fandango started, old warhorse," Fargo said to the Ovaro, grabbing leather and swinging up into the saddle again.

The trail to the top of the bluffs was nothing more than a series of narrow switchbacks formed over the years by snow runoff. Scree and glacial moraine were piled high on both sides, and Fargo knew he was a fish in a barrel if a hidden shooter wanted to drop a bead on him.

But six helpless kids, and a beautiful young temptress, pushed him on up the narrow trail. Now Fargo depended on all of his senses, and especially those of the Ovaro. Death lurked at each corkscrew turn, so Fargo instantly steeled his muscles for action when the pinto suddenly raised his head, ears pricked.

"What's on the spit?" Fargo said quietly, patting the Ovaro's neck to calm him.

The stallion's sensitive nostrils quivered, sampling the air. All horses feared the smell of bears, and the Ovaro also reacted to the Indian scent. But there was one other smell Fargo had taught the Ovaro to recognize—the distinctive odor of gun grease.

Thus alerted, Fargo now paid special attention to the rock abutment just above him—perfect cover for an ambush. Suddenly his goose tickle was back, tightening his scalp. Fargo was already rolling out of the saddle when he heard the telltale snick of a rifle being cocked.

The earsplitting crack of the first shot echoed off the surrounding rocks. Fargo felt a sharp tug at his buckskin shirt as the bullet passed harmlessly through the folds near his left armpit. He hit the rocky trail hard, landing on his left shoulder and hip. His Colt was already to hand, but so far he had no target.

Nor did the hidden marksman let up. Again and again he levered and fired, bullets whanging off the rocks all around Fargo. The well trained Ovaro began to back down the trail, refusing to run away completely without Fargo. But the packhorse went wild, bucking, jackknifing, crow-hopping.

And inevitably, given the wild spray of bullets, one of them caught the packhorse in the right flank, dropping it to its front knees.

Fargo cursed, knowing he'd play hell freeing those packs if that big horse fell over on its side. He hated wasting lead with no clear target. But he had no choice but to rapidly empty his six-shooter in the general direction of the rock abutment, hoping to force his attacker to momentarily cover down.

At least his action bought a few precious seconds. Realizing the packhorse was past help, Fargo quickly uncinched the packs of gold and heaved them onto the Ovaro. Then he jerked his Henry out of its scabbard and ended the gray's suffering with a quick shot to the brain.

By now the hidden rifleman had nerved up enough to start firing again. But Fargo had his Henry at the ready, and he traded bullet for bullet as he grabbed the Ovaro's bridle reins and began leading him quickly back down the trail. One round whizzed past so close it damn near parted Fargo's hair, and when it splattered into a boulder, rock dust flew in his eyes.

But abruptly the trail took a sharp dog-leg turn, and he and the Ovaro were momentarily safe.

"Whoever the hell you are, mister," Fargo roared out in a voice powerful enough to fill a canyon, "you just broke the rules! That gold's going to get buried now, in a place you'll never find without me! And you tell Danford this, you dry-gulching trash: Skye Fargo says he'll never see one red cent of that money if even one kid is hurt. That goes for the woman, too. Now we're playing by *my* rules, and you just remember—hell ain't even *half* full!"

5

With no possibility of riding up that steep trail to the top of the bluffs, Fargo played his only hand and retreated down to the tableland near the creek. Once he was screened by the timber north of the creek, he thumbed reloads into his Colt and the tube magazine of his Henry. Then he hastily dug out a wallow and covered the gold, piling plenty of brush and leaves over the spot.

Knowing his Ovaro was no help for the time being, Fargo threw the bridle, uncinched the saddle, then grained the stallion good before ground-hitching him on a long tether near graze and water, but hidden from above.

Then, staying in the trees, he spent at least an hour studying every inch of that steep bluff. And finally he found what he sought: an alternate way up.

It was a series of staircase ledges about three hundred yards to the left of the main trail. It would be a rough piece of work to make that climb, but it had to be done. A germ of a plan had formed in Fargo's mind, based on one main consideration: His tactics must not push Danford's gang to the point of killing any hostages.

As day bled into night, Fargo prepared his eyes for night vision by wrapping his blanket around his head for nearly an hour. The resulting total darkness dilated his pupils so much that, when he removed the blanket well after sunset, he could make out plenty of details despite the grainy darkness of the night.

He had already thoroughly cleaned his Henry. Now he rigged a crude sling on the rifle with a rawhide thong and slung it across his back. The climb up the face of the bluff went better than he had expected. His long arms and legs made it less difficult to reach hand and footholds, as did his increased night vision, which warned him away from numerous snake dens.

He had no clear idea exactly where he would emerge topside. When he did finally drag himself over the rim of the bluff, however, his mouth tugged itself into a surprised smile.

A half moon shimmered on a pine-sheltered pond where Kristen McKenna was standing with her back toward him. She was dressed in a simple blue gingham dress with a single flounce, bathing a couple of the smaller children.

"There you go, Ginny," she said in a soothing tone, briskly drying a cute little girl's wet mop of curls. "I know it's chilly, hon, but you'll warm up quick now that you're dry. Now, Sarah, you're the oldest. You take Ginny and Mattie back to the cave and get them tucked into their beds. Tell the boys I'll be along as soon as I take a quick bath. Then they can come and wash up. And tell Taffy I want him to stand guard. If any of those men, especially that Booth Collins, head toward the pond . . ."

She said no more to spare the younger girls. But Sarah was old enough to understand her fear.

"Don't you fret, Miz McKenna," Sarah responded. "If they do, I'll have Taffy sing 'Buffalo Gal' at the top of his lungs."

Fargo watched the trio of little girls troop dutifully back toward the cavern, holding hands. This reminder of their innocence strengthened his resolve as he thought about what Danford and his gang were doing to these kids. But strong emotions only got in the way of the senses, so he cleared his mind of all thought, staying alert and vigilant.

The surface of the water wrinkled gently when the breeze gusted, and falling pine needles had formed a soft carpet underfoot. Under different circumstances, the peaceful spot would seem like a little corner of paradise. For some time she just stood there, tears streaming down her cheeks, a sob occasionally hitching in her chest.

Then, all cried out for now, she decided a bracing bath in this clear but cold water might restore a little of her snap and vigor—and wash off the feeling of filth those men caused in her. Luckily, despite the current fashion rage among women for wearing wide and restrictive hoops, she had decided to leave her cumbersome "crinoline cage" back east. As a result, disrobing was much easier.

She glanced over her shoulder to make sure no one was spying. Then, quickly, she began to undo the buttons of her dress.

Gliding like a shadow, placing his feet carefully to avoid snapping any sticks, Fargo moved toward the pond as Kristen McKenna peeled off her clothing. He could hear horses snorting and stomping behind a distant line of aspen trees and made a mental map of the location—scattering those mounts would seriously hobble the Danford gang's escape plans.

He watched the curvaceous blonde leave her dress, petticoats, and pantaloons in a puddle around her well-turned ankles, stepping gingerly into the brisk water. Fargo had dallied with all sorts of females during his wanderings, and he found the fair sex too delightful to prefer any one type over another.

But if he had to hand out a blue ribbon for female frames, this gal would surely make the runoff. She definitely did not qualify for membership in the Itty Bitty Titty Club. Fargo had never seen breasts quite that large and heavy on such a slender-framed gal—breasts that, despite their sheer size and weight, rode high and proud, capped by huge, cocoa-colored aureoles and pert strawberry nipples that had stiffened against the cold.

She had let her hair down, and it fell over her shoulders in pale golden tresses. Her stomach was gently rounded, her hips wide and flaring. The silky, dark-blond "V" of mons hair looked like pure French wool. She turned her back for a moment, and he admired her taut butt, split high like a Georgia peach. And there were two fetching little dimples at the base of her spine.

As much as he was enjoying the show, Fargo needed to let this pretty and alluring reporter know that help was at hand. Without hope, she would either give up or do something desperately stupid. Yet, he dare not let her scream, alerting the others.

Kristen clutched her elbows against the night chill. She was just poking one tentative toe into the brisk pond water when Fargo seized her from behind, his right hand clamped over her mouth, his left just under the impressive heft of her breasts.

City lass Kristen McKenna fought like a hellcat unleashed, surprising Fargo with her strength. He restrained her mainly with his left arm, and although he had originally grabbed her around the stomach, her wild struggles resulted in repeatedly filling his hand with those delightful and magnificent breasts of hers. Nor could he ignore the taut firmness of her bare ass as it ground into the front of his trousers, causing twinges of excitement to take form beneath the buckskin.

"Damn it all, Miss McKenna," he hissed into her ear, "no need for the catfit, I ain't here to hurt you. My name is Skye Fargo, and I've been hired by the Northwestern Short Line to rescue you—if you don't claw my eyes out first."

Finally she got turned around enough to take a good look at him in the buttery moonlight. When she realized he wasn't one of her captors, here to outrage her, her eyes lit up like a prairie ablaze.

"I recognize you! You're the man who got shot off his horse yesterday when the train was derailed. And according to Danford, you rescued half the kids."

Fargo nodded, reluctantly letting her go. But he couldn't peel his eyes away from her magnificent, moonlit nakedness. She looked like an ivory goddess. In her initial relief at the prospect of rescue, she seemed to forget she wasn't wearing a stitch. Words started spurting out of her, so quickly she hardly paused for a breath.

"Oh, thank God! Mr. Fargo, the man in charge is a monster named Dakota Danford, and the men with him were all part of his ring when he was working for Overland Stage. He—"

"I already know all that," Fargo cut her off brusquely. "Danford figured he held the keys to the mint, and then the railroad bought up Overland and fired him and his lickspittles. What matters now is how we get you and the kids out of here safe."

Despite her fear and relief, Kristen was a "progressive, modern woman" from a prominent Manhattan family intimate with Astors and Vanderbilts. She was about fed up with insults and intimidation and rudeness from these rough frontier types, and that included the bearded, buckskin-clad man ogling her now. Fargo's rugged good looks and exciting masculine power aside, she resented his take-charge manner and tone. She was used to deferential, genteel men.

"Sir, I'll have you know I write for the *New York Herald*," she informed him archly. "Some call it the greatest newspaper in America."

"If it's a newspaper, I call it a crapsheet. Today's headlines wipe tomorrow's butts. Don't high-hat me, lady. Look around you—this ain't your damned bass-ackwards city full of store-fed clerks and psalm singers. Out here in the high lonesome, sugar plum, the cow don't bellow to the bull."

Her big, almond-shaped eyes grew even bigger with indignation. "There's plenty of *bull*, all right! You take that superior tone with me, and yet—why, have you ever translated a passage of Latin? Would you even recognize a Greek hexameter? How dare you?"

But Fargo was very well educated on the subject of shutting up mouthy females who delivered windy lectures at moments of danger. Especially when they stood bare-butt naked before him.

"Best way to cure a boil," he muttered, "is to lance it."

She froze when Fargo shrugged the rifle off his back—was he going to shoot her for speaking out? But he propped it against a nearby tree and suddenly crushed the naked woman in a strong embrace, lifting her clear off the ground and possessing her mouth with his.

For a moment, taken by surprise, she briefly resisted. But then it was as if a passion dam broke within her, releasing the fear and loneliness of the past two days. Right now, more than anything else, she needed to stop thinking, fretting, fearing. Her hungry and greedy tongue sparred with his, probing, tasting, igniting a fire in the loins of both of them.

"Damn," Fargo said on a sigh as their mouths parted, "you got a short fuse, girl, though that ain't a complaint."

Kristen cupped both huge, creamy, plum-tipped breasts and pushed them toward him.

Fargo was more than happy to oblige her. He lowered his mouth onto first one, then the other, sucking and licking them stiff. Now and then he added a light nibble with his teeth, just enough to make her whimper encouragement. Only a minute or so of this, and she was hotter than a branding iron.

Kristen boldly untied his trousers and let them drop, stepping back a bit to stare at his exposed manhood in the shimmering moonlight. She seemed mesmerized by his startling thickness and length, and the way his shaft leaped with each heartbeat—a magnificent battle lance ready for action.

"My goodness!" she marveled when she could trust her voice again. "Have you ever hurt a girl with that . . . big thing?"

"Hurt? I've had no complaints on that score," he replied teasingly, rolling her nipples between his forefingers and thumbs. "But quite a few of them have screamed and groaned."

"I'll just bet they have."

He grinned. "I guess you writers got a way with words."

"And what are *you* good at besides sneaking up on a lady?"

"Oh, this and that."

"That's fine," she said in a hot, breathy voice that tickled his ear when she moved real close. "Because you want *this*—"

She grabbed one of his hands and guided it to the warm, wet petals and folds of her sex. Fargo felt an extra surge of lust when he realized how hot and lathered he had her already. Even her satiny inner thighs were slick with her brimming desire.

"—and I want *that*," she concluded, gripping his shaft and beginning to stroke him. "They should be introduced."

Fargo fully agreed, especially when she gave him an extra little squeeze that made his legs go wobbly with desire. But he couldn't help casting a wary glance toward the cave.

"Don't worry," Kristen urged, tugging him down onto the soft carpet of pine needles. "A very sharp young lad named Taffy is keeping watch for me. He'll start singing 'Buffalo Gal' if any of the men head this way."

Fargo required no further urging. He placed one hand on each of her thighs and spread her open wide. Kristen was indeed a progressive girl. Boldly she seized his curving shaft and held it at the perfect angle, so that one good flex of his hips sent him plunging deep into the hottest, wettest depths of her.

Within mere moments she turned into a tiger in a whirlwind. Only by quickly covering her mouth again with kisses did Fargo prevent her from crying out in passionate abandon, so unbridled was her lustful need. He thrust deep and hard, their hips instinctively finding a perfect rhythm. She wasn't the kind who just laid there like a wooden Indian and let the man do all the erotic acrobatics. She wiggled and trembled and drove him to a frenzy of pleasure as she milked his manhood with her talented love muscle, squeezing his length over and over until he felt a volcanic eruption building in his loins.

She raised both long, shapely legs and locked them behind his back, wanting every last centimeter of him.

"Oh, Skye, you're so big it feels like you're up to my belly button! Oh, lord, Skye! I'm gonna—oh, I'm gonna—I'm gonna . . . ex*plode*!" she cried out, and she did, over and over in powerful waves, each climax more overwhelming than the one before it.

She was still bucking and writhing when Fargo moved his hands under her taut ass and lifted her to him even tighter. Like a masterful stallion he gave several powerful, conclusive thrusts, spending himself deep inside her.

The intensity of their passion, and its explosive release, left them both dazed and drifting, limbs still entwined. Then, above the quiet soughing of the wind in the pines, came a sound that slapped them back to harsh reality. A young boy's slightly reedy voice, singing loudly and a little desperately:

> *Buffalo Gal, won't you come out tonight,*
> *Come out tonight,*
> *Come out tonight . . . ?*

"Hush that damn caterwauling, you little popinjay," Booth Collins snapped, slapping Taffy hard. "Getcher skinny ass back inside the cave pronto or I'll whip the snot outta you, boy."

"Rot in hell, gourd ear!" Taffy sassed back. He knew it was risky, but he wanted the killer's mind on him, not on that nice Miss McKenna. So he sat there defiantly, scowling at his tormentor.

Collins advanced toward him, big and menacing in the silvery moonlight. "So you think you got a set on you, hanh? You mouthy pup, I'll—"

Dakota Danford stepped outside the cave and placed a restraining hand on Collins's shoulder.

"Damnit, kid," Danford snapped at Taffy, "don't sit there eyeballing us like some stupid mooncalf. Stir your stumps! Get inside and stay there."

Taffy scowled at them, but did what he was told.

"What are you frettin' and steamin' about now?" Danford demanded when they were alone. "Are you so damned thin-skinned that a city runt can get your dander up?"

"Well, I'm sick of those damn brats lally-laggin' around, is all. Put 'em to work."

But Collins spoke absently, for his mind, and eyes, were directed toward the pond hidden behind the pine trees. That McKenna gal was out there right now, maybe bare-assed naked. . . .

"You know, Danford," he remarked, "when a man's on the dodge like we are, it gets mighty boring of a night."

"Just put that woman away from your thoughts, Booth, you hear me? Now ain't the time for that."

"You tellin' me *you* ain't diddled her yet?" Collins demanded.

"No, and you won't neither, not yet. Once you boys get that first taste of her, you'll all be useless to me. You'll end up like a pack of snarling curs, fightin' over who gets her next. A man with ruttin' on his mind is worthless in a sudden scrape. I want your mind on Skye Fargo. You heard that message he gave Nash for us. It's a cinch bet he won't give up easy. Twice now we've sent lead flying at him, and he's still above the ground."

"Skye Fargo is chicken fixins," Collins jeered, still staring toward the pond with sick, hungry intensity.

"The hell he is. He's left a trail of graves behind him filled with cocky bastards like you."

"You 'member Reno Sloan?" Collins demanded. "That famous killer from the Black Rock Desert country? He had every swinging dick west of Omaha quaking in their boots.

Even the Ute Injins, no tribe to fool with, called him bad medicine and steered wide of him. But I braced him in Miles City and planted two slugs in his belly 'fore he even cleared leather. Don't you fret no living legends. Skye Fargo bleeds red like all the rest, and I mean to see he dies hard."

"Fargo ain't a hired gun, Booth, he's a lone wolf, a tracker, and a survivor. It ain't just your fancy quick draw and circus shooting that keeps a man alive. Besides, he *ain't* gonna die until we got that gold, and that's an order."

"If I see him," Collins insisted, "I'm filling his belly with lead."

"Like hell you are! If you got a sliver in your finger, do you cut your arm off at the elbow? Sure he's got you riled, but *he's got our gold*. Besides, he ain't got a chance in hell unless he cuts a deal with us. My cousin Red is still on our side, remember that. And Fargo, hell, he's trapped down there on the flats. That dead horse chokes the trail, plus we got Nash and Heck posted on guard. And even if all hell does break loose, we got us a fast way out that nobody knows about."

"So what do we do in the meantime?" Collins snapped. "Sit and play a harp until Fargo's ready to make medicine? I'm gettin' holed-up fever in that damn cave."

"So what? This is *gold*, damnit! Good coin of the realm anyplace in the world. Not a man jack one of us will ever have to work again, not the way money stretches in Old Mexico. It'll be whores and liquor and cards for us. And fancy silver-trimmed duds like them dons wear—hell, I might even start me up one a them whatchacallits, them haciendas and just fill it up with pretty whores."

"You keep harping away on them soiled doves in Mexico," Collins cut in angrily, "when we got us a fine-lookin', tart-mouth little hussy right now."

"Damnit, Booth, I admit you're death to the devil with that short iron. But you're poor shakes when it comes to tactics. Now don't push me no more about the woman. I told you—"

"Take the pine cone outta your sitter. I give you my word I won't douse Fargo's light until we got the swag. But you harken and heed, Dakota—far as that woman is concerned, you can stick your tactics where the sun don't shine. On account I'm goin' out to spark that little city princess right now. And God help any fool that comes twixt this dog and his meat."

Collins dropped his hand onto the butt of his .38 to underscore his resolve.

Danford quickly weighed all his options and decided to give in this time. Booth Collins was mouthy and hard to control, but exactly the kind of flint-hearted, steel-nerved killer Danford wanted on his side.

"All right," he finally gave in. "But at least don't tell Nash and Heck about it."

Collins grinned, hitching his shell belt. "To hear you take on about it, you'd think she was your sister. But don't fret, mum's the word."

He started walking toward the dark mass of the pines.

"I mean it, Booth," Danford flung after him. "I ain't runnin' no cathouse here. Do it out there by the pond, and if she starts to scream—"

"She'll be quiet," Collins assured him. "Or elsewise she'll be *real* quiet."

The moment she heard Taffy start singing, Kristen McKenna broke into a panic.

"Skye! Oh, my stars! That's the signal! That means—"

"Shush it," he cut her off, leaping to his feet and pulling up his trousers. "Just stay quiet and get dressed quick as you can. Nobody's going to hurt you."

His calm manner and tone worked like a tonic on her nerves, calming her as she followed his orders. Despite her fear, the pleasure of their intense coupling still lingered. As she hurriedly finished dressing, she sent him a low-lidded smile.

Fargo hefted his rifle, but only to sling it across his back again for the climb down the bluff. Meanwhile, his trail-honed ears were listening for the new arrival's footsteps, gauging the man's distance. Still at least forty yards off, he judged, and moving in slow and sneaky, as rapists will.

"It's most likely Booth Collins," she whispered as she quickly slid her feet into her side-buttoning boots. "Are you going to . . . kill him?"

"Distinct possibility," he replied. "But not now."

Keeping one ear cocked to the approaching danger,

speaking in hushed tones, Fargo quickly explained their dilemma. He couldn't simply start picking Danford's gang off one by one, for fear of retaliation against the kids or Kristen. So, until the right opportunity presented itself, he must settle for keeping the gang nervous, wondering, jumping at every noise and shadow. Push them enough to keep their nerves stretched, but not hard enough to kill anybody. This would be more like Indian-style harassment: surprise and mystify your enemy, strike quick from ambush, wage a war of nerves.

And although he didn't mention it now to Kristen, Fargo had another motivation for buying a little time—he hoped to prove a link between Danford and his cousin, Sheriff Red Bolton. That was one reason why Fargo had enlisted the eyes and ears of Danny Ford and Owen Maitland back in Bear Creek.

"You go back to the cave by your usual path," he instructed the pretty reporter. "Give me thirty seconds head start, then head back."

"But what about—?"

He kissed the protest off her lips. "No need to fret. Our sneaky friend will get back before you do, I promise. From now on, listen for the hooting of an owl—that'll be me telling you that I'm out here. Oh, one more thing. Keep your eyes peeled inside the cave. I got a gut hunch there's a secret way out."

"A hunch? But—"

"Darlin', why would Danford pick a spot like this? Sure, it's a safe location for a short time, long as you're provisioned. But it also turns into a deathtrap if your pursuers decide to surround you in a siege, cutting off your supply line. It doesn't add up, somehow, unless there's a hidden way out. Now remember, count to thirty after I leave, then get back to the cave."

Fargo lit out fast in the direction of the approaching noises, not being at all quiet, that was part of his plan. In fact, he deliberately thrashed straight through some underbrush, raising plenty of racket.

Fargo heard the unmistakable metallic click of a hammer being thumbed back to full cock.

"Who is that?" a nervous male voice challenged. "That you, cottontail, stuck in the bushes?"

Fargo grabbed a small tree branch and snapped it off loudly, using it to thrash some more underbrush.

"I said who is that?"

Fargo had spent most of his life wandering the frontier, learning its many lessons. And one lesson he had learned well was how to recognize the distinctive woofing sound of a foraging bear, a strange, deep noise halfway between a grunt and a growl.

"Woof!" he coughed out now, making the explosive sound from deep in his belly. *"Woof, woof!"*

Collins, or whoever was out there, evidently knew the sound too, for he suddenly opened fire. Several bullets hummed past Fargo's position, one uncomfortably close.

But only a fool counted on a handgun to drop a bear, especially a brown bear or a grizzly. And Collins was no fool. Fargo grinned when he heard the frightened man running back toward the cave, cursing loudly when he stumbled.

Fargo immediately headed for the lip of the bluff, planning to climb back down into the timber before the gang had a chance to look around.

Scattering those hidden horses, he told himself regretfully, would have to wait for another time. Nor could these Indian tricks guarantee victory, only buy some time.

Right now he had six innocent kids and a beautiful, spirited young woman right in the line of fire. But once they were all safe, he meant to give the out-of-work Danford gang some brand-new jobs—shoveling coal in hell.

6

Skye Fargo spent the rest of the night camped on a bench of grass beside Cheyenne Creek. He slept for only a few hours, using his saddle for a pillow.

Just before dawn he rolled up his blanket and ground sheet, shivering a little—there was still a snap to the air of a morning. He was so hungry his stomach wouldn't stop rumbling. It turned out he had lost his provisions during the ambush attempt yesterday.

He knew he could make a meal of a prairie chicken, plentiful in this area. But he didn't want to fire a weapon and reveal his position to the gang on the bluff. And setting a snare would take too much time. So instead, he split open a buffalo-leg bone he'd found earlier and made do with the nutritious marrow.

Fargo knew he had to ride back to Middle Fork Creek to check the lightning-split tree for any messages from town. First, however, he took advantage of the first gray light of day to carefully reconnoiter his position. By now he figured there were others gunning for him besides Danford's crew of cutthroats.

Leaving the Ovaro tethered in the trees, he scouted the area on foot. Just beyond the woods he found plenty of fresh tracks and horse droppings, confirming that somebody, most likely Red Bolton's men, was prowling around looking for him. They had been riding after dark. He surmised that from the number of rocks that were turned over, rocks a horse would have avoided in daylight. And a few of the horse droppings were even still slightly warm. That meant trouble might be lurking close by—lethally close.

One vital task remained. Fargo carefully examined the

pinto's feet and hooves for embedded stones or thorns. A horse gone lame, on the open plains or in hostile surroundings, meant almost certain trouble. A man could clean his weapons until they sparkled. But let his horse founder, and he was marked for burial by the buzzards.

Satisfied the stallion was sound of foot, Fargo rode out from the trees about an hour after sunup, bearing due south toward Middle Fork Creek. A sense of urgency made him urge the well rested Ovaro to a hard run, for time was pushing against him. This would be the second full day for the captives. The more time that passed, the greater the danger that those thugs would grow desperate.

At least, Fargo consoled himself, Danford's bunch still believed they occupied an impregnable position, one he couldn't breach except by the main trail. Perhaps that mistaken assumption would make them careless.

Nor were all his thoughts gloomy and unpleasant. Fleeting memories of a naked Kristen McKenna, working him into a lather with those gyrating hips of hers, coaxed a little smile onto his lips. Lord but that little city filly was hot to trot. . . .

"What man has done," he promised himself out loud, "man will do." One roll in the hay, with a little firecracker like her, just wasn't enough.

Unfortunately, the message waiting for him in the lightning-split tree cooled his warm blood in a hurry.

The note was scrawled on the back of an old calendar page. Young Danny Ford wasn't much of a speller, but he got right to the point clear enough:

> Trubble in town. Get hear quik. But watch for amboosh from Boltons bunch.

Who else but Cousin Red, Fargo thought grimly as he pointed the Ovaro's bridle toward the town of Bear Creek. Danny's warning about a possible ambush was no doubt accurate, but unnecessary—it had become second nature for the Trailsman to be prepared for the unexpected.

He followed a narrow freight road first established for resupply of Fort Laramie, constantly scanning the surrounding slopes and rock formations. Fargo was perhaps two miles north of town, still searching carefully for the

55

reflected glint of rifle barrels, when something flashed in the corner of his right eye.

He tugged rein, veering off the wagon-rutted road and slipping behind a low ridge beside it. The brief flash of light had come from the top of a knoll about three hundred yards ahead. There were rocks up there, so Fargo knew it might simply have been the sun flashing off quartz or mica. But a man stayed above the ground by assuming the worst.

He ground-hitched the Ovaro and quickly hooked around behind the knoll, moving through a cutbank to keep himself hidden. A few minutes later he spotted a chestnut gelding with a roached mane, hobbled well behind the knoll. And beyond the horse, just beneath the crown of the knoll, he spotted a crouching man wearing a sturdy hopsack coat.

The man, armed with a buffalo gun, was anxiously craning his neck in every direction, trying to figure out where Fargo had gone. The Trailsman knocked the thong off the hammer of his Colt, then drew the weapon and thumb-cocked it.

"Drop that Big Fifty and grab some sky, mister!" Fargo called out behind him. "Then turn around mighty damn slow, or I'll burn you where you stand."

Fargo's voice carried its own authority. The would-be bushwhacker did as told. The moment he turned around, Fargo recognized him as one of Bolton's tinhorn deputies. In fact, the same one who had tried to threaten him two days earlier in the saloon with "friendly advice."

Fargo said, "You could've knocked me out of the saddle at a thousand yards with that buff gun, but you didn't. That means you're under orders to take me alive. So Red Bolton already knows I hid that gold, huh?"

"Stranger, you're babbling six ways to Sunday. I'm just out doin' a little huntin' to put meat on the table."

"Yeah, just like I'm bunking with Queen Victoria. Butt your saddle, mister. I'm taking you to Fort Laramie under citizen's arrest. I know they can't hold you long since the murder didn't happen. But the C.O. there is a friend of mine. He'll keep you in the stockade for awhile on my say-so. Maybe we'll make it more permanent later."

Fargo stepped aside to let the man return to his horse.

Something shifty and furtive in the prisoner's eyes warned Fargo he was about to try something stupid.

Fargo wagged the Colt for emphasis. "I got six beans in the wheel, old son, and I'm already tickling the trigger. Don't sull on me."

The man placed his left foot in the stirrup. "Now, you just look-a-here, mister. . . ."

But the talk was only a distraction. Quick as a striking snake, Bolton's toady whipped out a boot gun. However, Fargo had the reflexes of a cat. His first slug drilled the man through the heart and knocked him ass-over-applecart, one foot still twisted into the stirrup.

"That was your call, fellow," Fargo said to deaf ears. "But we all got to die once, I expect."

He took no pleasure in the killing and regretted the man's stupidity. But Fargo also knew the bloodletting was far from over.

He slung the body over the chestnut, retrieved the Big Fifty, then led the horse back toward the spot where he'd left his Ovaro.

Time to pay a little visit to Red Bolton. And leave him a calling card to prove Skye Fargo meant to play this game through to the end.

Red Bolton was seated behind a battered kneehole desk, sorting through a stack of reward dodgers, when Fargo entered his office. The self-appointed sheriff glanced up just in time to watch Fargo unceremoniously drop a dead body onto the floor in front of the desk.

Bolton's eyes bulged out like wet, white marbles. His granite-hard features registered shock, and his face went as pale as putty behind the dark longhorn mustache.

"Generally, it's my policy to bury a fellow human being," Fargo informed him. "But this one don't qualify, so he's your headache."

Bolton sat frozen for a few heartbeats. Then he scraped back his chair and walked around the desk to stare at the corpse.

"That's Deuce Longstreet," he finally said, staring at Fargo. "He was one of my deputies."

"That the best you can say about him?"

"Fargo, you'll swing for this!"

Bolton slapped for his six-shooter, but Fargo stopped his arm with a grip like an eagle's talon.

"You'd best brush up on territorial law, *sheriff*. Notice the bullet hole is in the front. If there's no witness against a man, and the hole's in front, it's ruled a justified killing. If that short iron of yours clears leather, there'll be another legal killing, and Bear Creek will be rid of one more crooked lawman."

Bolton's face bloated with purple rage. "You strutting son of a bitch! You was hired by the railroad to fetch them kids back, not kill my deputies."

Fargo shrugged one shoulder, keeping a close eye on Bolton. "When a man is ordered to waylay me, I tend to take it real personal like. I gave him the chance to live, but he pushed his luck. Better tell the rest of your roaches to stay in the woodwork, or they'll get stepped on, too."

"That tears it," Bolton muttered, unbuckling his gun belt and tossing it onto the desk. "Fargo, you're overdue for an ass whipping."

Fargo dropped his own belt. "Let's get thrashing."

Fargo had a slight reach advantage, but Bolton had thirty pounds on him, most of it solid muscle. He was also a man who fought from temper, not tactics, and Fargo had learned from hard experience how best to square off with a raging bull.

Bolton started off by savagely hurling his chair at Fargo, who sidestepped it by inches. Then he simply lunged at Fargo, fists the size of Virginia hams swinging wildly and finding nothing but air. Fargo deftly avoided them, letting Bolton wear himself down with empty swings while also beating at his face, ribs, and stomach with quick, hard jabs.

Fargo was momentarily slowed by a potbellied stove, and Bolton connected a hard left just in front of his ear. The Trailsman staggered but kept his footing, then launched back with a series of rapid one-two punches that rattled Bolton. Before he could recover and attack again, Fargo finished him off with a powerful haymaker. It didn't knock Bolton out, but it dropped him to his knees, eyes glazed.

"Skye Fargo! Skye, is that you raising all that ruckus?"

The voice came from behind the raw plank door leading

58

to the cells. Fargo recognized it immediately: Owen Maitland, the surveyor.

Keeping a weather eye on Bolton, Fargo stepped to the door. It was locked, but a glance through the Judas hole showed him Maitland in one of the cells. Usually neat as a pin, now there were haggard pockets under his eyes, and his face bristled with whiskers. There was also a big, grape-colored bruise covering one side of his face.

So this is why Danny called me back to town, Fargo thought.

"The hell's this all about, Bolton?" Fargo demanded.

By now the head of the Bear Creek Vigilance Committee had regained at least some of his usual swaggering confidence. He slowly struggled to his feet, then stood with both boots planted wide and his thumbs hooked into his shell belt. But a swollen lip and bloody nose detracted from his tough stance.

"He tried to rape a dime-a-dance gal from the Last Alibi saloon."

"That's a cock-and-bull story and you know it. Owen Maitland wouldn't swat a fly. What evidence you got?"

Bolton smirked, enjoying this immensely. "That ain't none a your bee's wax, Fargo. But I'll tell you anyhow. I got a sworn statement from the lady herself. And two witnesses."

"Let me guess—two more of your penny-ante deputies?"

"That's the fall of the cards. A witness is a witness."

"What's the lady's name?" Fargo demanded.

"None of your god—"

"Her name is Dusty Robinson!" Owen shouted through the door. "If she's not working, her room is behind the saloon."

"Shut your cake hole, Maitland!" Bolton yelled back. "Or I'll shut it for you!"

Fargo, never once showing his back to Bolton, strapped his gun back on and headed toward the street door. "I'll put it to you straight, Bolton. You lay a hand on him again, and I'll have your guts for garters. What I just gave you was only a taste. That's a cast-iron guarantee."

"Rot in hell, you meddling bastard! I'll piss on your grave yet, Fargo!"

The Trailsman, one hand on the latch-string, stared the other man down. "You don't have the stones for it, Bolton. You're a back-shooting coward. Won't be long, and I'll link you with your cousin and the kidnappings. And then you'll all stretch hemp."

"You're just shooting at rovers," Bolton blustered. "You got any proof I'm involved? Or even that my cousin is mixed up in it?"

Fargo looked at him as if Bolton were something nasty he had just scraped off his boot. "I plan to provide plenty of proof. A lot more than you needed to frame Owen. But I got a gut-hunch it may never get to court in your case—no point in hanging a dead man, is there?"

Business at the Last Alibi saloon was slow at this early hour. The friendly bartender told Fargo the dance girls wouldn't show up for a few hours yet.

Keeping an eye peeled in every direction, Fargo circled around to the back of the dilapidated building. He knocked on the door the bartender had directed him to. He felt hidden eyes on him, but doubted anyone would shoot him, not with that gold secretly stashed away.

"Who is it?" a female voice called out.

"Skye Fargo, Dusty."

"Mister, I dance with men for money, but that's *all* I do with them. Please go away. There's a sporting house in Laramie."

"Darlin', I never pay a lady for her favors, that takes the fun right out of it. But I'm not here for that. I need to talk with you."

"I'm sorry, I'm not feeling well," the voice called back, muffled by the door. She sounded scared.

"Dusty, I'm not one to bully a lady. And I'm *not* here to hurt you. But I'm also not letting Owen Maitland face prison time for a crime you and I both know he never committed. Now, either you open that door or I'll have to kick it down."

A few moments later a bolt shot open, and Fargo was looking down into the honey-colored eyes of a petite woman in her mid-twenties, wrapped in a yellow chenille robe. Dusty Robinson was a timid, pretty girl with dark brown hair hanging in sausage curls.

"Well, then. Come on in," she said reluctantly, her eyes fleeing from his.

She was obviously frightened that someone was watching. Fargo stepped into a small, clean room with a rose-patterned carpet and a few sticks of simple furniture. A painting of the Madonna and child, in a giltwood frame, hung over the narrow iron bedstead in one corner.

She started to turn quickly away, but he caught her gently by the shoulders. Fargo cupped her chin and turned her face to study the slight swelling along her jawline.

"Who hit you? Bolton or one of his dirt-workers?"

"I don't know what you mean, Mr. Fargo. I—I simply slipped on some stairs."

"Pretty clumsy footwork for a gal who dances for a living. Don't try to bamboozle me, honey. You're scared spitless. Bolton forced you to sign a complaint against Owen, didn't he? Why?"

Nervously, she nibbled on a sliver of cuticle, unable to meet his gaze. A tear suddenly rolled down her cheek.

"Red Bolton said he'd kill me," she finally blurted out. "Kill me if I didn't swear out the complaint. Mr. Maitland does sort of, well, like me. But he has never disrespected me or any woman in this town. Why, he's one of the few true gentlemen. It's just—he was caught in the saloon eavesdropping on some of Bolton's men. Oh, Mr. Fargo, they'll *kill* me, I just know—"

He firmed his grip on her shoulders to calm her. "Ain't nobody going to hurt you, I'll see to that. I'll be back in a little bit. Just lock the door and wait for me."

Fargo paid a visit to Peyton Norwood at the office of the Northwestern Short Line. He briefed the worried railroad executive on the situation at Devil's Catacombs and the developments here in town. Norwood seemed reluctant to believe Red Bolton was in on the plot. But he was taking plenty of heat from the press and his superiors back in Omaha, so he readily agreed to Fargo's requests. The pale clerk in the green eyeshades quickly drew up the document Fargo dictated to him, then drew up a file copy for the office safe.

"Take this," Fargo told Dusty when he returned.

He handed her a bank draft drawn on the Omaha Commerce Bank and signed by Norwood. "There's a boarding

61

house in the settlement near Fort Laramie. Stay there until all this blows over. You know Danny Ford?"

She nodded. "Nice kid."

"I'll make arrangements to have him stop by soon with a conveyance. Once I know you're safely underway, I'll be taking this over to Red Bolton's office. You'll need to read and sign it first."

He showed her the document the clerk had drawn up in painfully neat letters, the ink expertly blotted with fine sand. It was a statement clearing Owen Maitland on the grounds that she had mistaken her attacker's identity in a state of nervous excitement. It explicitly stated that she was pressing no charges.

When she looked up, hesitant, Fargo said, "Dusty, can you live with yourself if Owen goes to prison?"

Her eyes cut to the picture over her bed, and a new resolve came into her eyes. She fetched a steel nib and a pot of ink from the highboy beside her bed.

"No, I can't," she replied, signing the document. "I'm ashamed I even considered it."

"It was fear made you do it," Fargo assured her. "Under the circumstances, you had little choice."

"Red Bolton has terrorized this area long enough. You're a stranger, yet you are willing to fight him. It's about time those of us who live here showed some backbone, too. I'll pack some things and wait for Danny."

She signed the document. As Fargo turned to leave, she impulsively rose up on tiptoe and kissed his cheek.

"Last Sunday at church," she told him, "Reverend Peabody said, 'A man brave for one second can change the course of history.' I think you've been brave all your life. I see it in your face, your eyes, the way you carry yourself. Maybe the Lord sent you to us, Skye, to change things around here. But *please* be careful. The men you're up against are ruthless and cunning. The Lord may be on your side, but Bolton and Danford have all the devils in hell on theirs."

7

Skye Fargo, Kristen McKenna told herself, was much more than just a ruggedly handsome man and a superb lover. He might not know how to read Greek and Latin, but he had certainly mastered the art of frontier survival. And the art of reading the criminal mind. His prediction was coming true: the four men holding her and the kids were getting worried and jumpy.

Even Booth Collins had lost much of his interest in sexually tormenting her, too busy worrying about his own skin. As time dragged by, between Fargo and that gold eluding them, the men were losing confidence. They were keeping two sentries on guard at all times now. But Kristen had finally overheard enough to know that Skye's instincts were right in hiding that gold.

The minute Danford laid hands on it, she and the kids were doomed. Danford wanted more than wealth. He was a vengeful monster, and he wanted their deaths blamed on the railroad barons who had sent him packing. A rescue of the captives would accomplish just the opposite by making the railroad bosses look like "good guys." Danford wouldn't stand for that.

Kristen and the children currently had the cave to themselves. Dakota Danford stood just outside the cave entrance shaving, using a mirror nailed to a tree. Even with shaving soap covering his face, he still smoked one of his stinky Mexican cigars. Now and then he glanced into the cave to check on her. Those deep-sunk eyes like cold flint sent a tingling shudder down her spine.

Twelve-year-old Sarah sat down beside Kristen, her face pale with nervous strain. Her little sister, Mattie, had never been a strong child. This terrible ordeal was only making matters worse.

"Mattie's burning up with fever," Sarah reported in a hushed tone. "She needs a doctor, Miss McKenna. Or at least some medicine."

"If only I had remembered to pack some quinine," Kristen fretted. "Ginny has developed a cough, too. It's this damp air."

Kristen could see the rest of the kids from where she sat on her straw bed near the back of the cavern. Nick and his friend Liam were half-heartedly taking turns spinning a wooden top on a flat slab of stone. Ginny and Mattie each lay on their dirty straw shakedowns, both so young their cheeks were still plump with baby fat. Poor little Ginny still hadn't uttered a peep. She had taken refuge deep inside herself, and Kristen feared she might never speak again.

Only the oldest, Taffy, seemed to be holding up well—even defiantly. He was determined to protect Kristen and the younger kids, protect them with his life if need be. He had been toughened by all those nights he had slept outside, along the docks of Manhattan's East River, in the cruel heart of the New York winters. The cities, too, were wild frontiers for a homeless waif.

Tears threatened, but Kristen clenched her will like a fist, resisting them. She was all these kids had to cling to, and she must stay strong for their sakes. Thank God Skye was out there somewhere, or she wouldn't have the strength to soldier on.

"I'm afraid all I have are some headache powders," Kristen told Sarah. "But let's look again anyway."

When she was snatched from the train three days ago, Kristen had managed to grab her valise containing personal items. And a leather carrying case with part of the photographic equipment she'd brought along to document the kids' stories. Of course the men had already rifled through all of it, looking for valuables.

"Nothing useful," she affirmed, sorting through the valise. "But here, honey. At least take this handkerchief and soak it in water. You can put it on Mattie's forehead and fan her for a few minutes. Perhaps that'll cool her down a little."

Kristen started to snap shut the brass clasp of the valise. Then she remembered the small, secret side pocket hidden by the lining. The men had missed it when they pawed through the contents.

Her heart skipped a beat as she realized the hidden pocket contained a loaded British two-shot derringer. They were known as "muff guns" in London, where ladies carried them after dark for protection. Her well-meaning editor at the *New York Herald* had insisted she take it along.

Should I voluntarily surrender it to Danford, she wondered. After all, she could hardly take on four heavily armed men with only two bullets. How would they react if they found it now?

Sarah stood up to return to her sister. She clutched her elbows and shivered.

"B-r-r-r! There's a cold draft in this spot," she remarked before she left.

Kristen had noticed that, too—a cool, steady stream of air that blew from the shadowed back wall of the cavern. The wall appeared to be solid rock. But she remembered what Skye had suggested. There must be some secret way out of here.

She felt a sudden surge of hope. If Skye was right, that tunnel or connecting cave, or whatever it might be, was perhaps their only chance to live. Even a slim hope was at least something to cling to.

Kristen, keeping a wary eye on Danford, stood up and began to explore the seemingly solid wall of sedimentary shale. Now she noticed, deep in the murky shadows, a narrow fold or cleft. . . .

"Pssst!"

The warning came from Taffy, who was keeping watch as usual. Kristen barely managed to return to her spot before Dakota Danford and Booth Collins stepped inside.

"Pipe down, bawl-baby!" Collins snapped at little Mattie, who felt so ill she was quietly crying. "You, pip-squeak," he added, talking to Nick. "Fetch me a dipper of water pronto or I'll plant a boot up your skinny ass."

Kristen felt a surge of anger. "You're a big man, aren't you, Collins? Pushing kids around and bullying women. I wonder how tough you are when you're face-to-face with a *real* man?"

She regretted the remark immediately when both men sent suspicious stares her way.

"You got somebody partic'lar in mind?" Danford demanded.

She wisely held her tongue.

"I'll tell you this much, sugar britches," Danford added. "A 'real man' named Skye Fargo had best cough up that gold, and mighty damn quick, or one of these snot-drippers is gonna hang by their thumbs."

By now Nick was returning from the water bucket with the drink for Collins. The leg that had been injured years earlier made him limp noticeably, spilling a little water.

"Boy," Collins taunted with mean sarcasm, "you hobble like a cow with rickets, you know that? If I had a worthless whelp like you, I'd brain him against a tree."

Nick was only ten years old, but he tolerated no remarks from anyone about his injured leg. He already resented being ordered around. His young face a sudden mask of hurt dignity, he flung the water in Booth Collins's face. "Kiss a chicken on the lips, you blowhard!"

Collins, snarling with rage, lunged at the boy. A moment later, however, he howled in pain as Taffy bounced a rock off his back.

"Leave Nick alone, you stinking son of a bitch!" Taffy shouted. "You oughta talk—that ugly ear of yours would make a Bowery rat puke!"

Collins would have shot Taffy on the spot if Danford, the stronger of the two men, hadn't stayed his hand.

"Ease off, Booth," he snapped. "Cripesakes, lettin' them little pissants rile you like that! We got bigger fish to fry. Now get outside and give the hail to Nash, then go relieve him when he gets here. I got a job for him."

Reluctantly, Booth followed orders. But first he stared at Taffy with murder in his mean, predatory eyes.

"You mouthy little bastard, you're *mine*, hear me? I *will* bury you up to your neck in a red-ant mound, you sawed-off city runt."

After Collins left, Danford ordered Kristen and the kids outside. She understood now why he did this from time to time: Whatever job he had for Nash Johnson, it involved that secret way out.

A few minutes later Nash showed up, his Volcanic repeater tucked under his arm.

"Get a message to Red," Danford ordered him. "We're s'posed to be using mirror signals, but he ain't flashed me none. Find out what the hell's going on in Bear Creek and whether or not they've captured Fargo yet. Tell Red this waiting around shit is for the birds. And if you spot Fargo, do *not* kill him or our cake is dough. He's the only one knows where that gold is."

Johnson nodded. A moment later, almost like magic, he disappeared through the back wall of the cave.

"By Godfrey, I seen it all, Skye," reported Slappy Hupenbecker. "Poor Owen Maitland! Red Bolton conked him on the noggin with a barrel stave, laid him out cold. Owen, a rapist? That's a hoot! Red trumped up that charge to keep Owen locked up away from you. On account Owen's heard too much of their plans."

Slappy paused to take out his plug and slice a chaw off it. When he had it cheeked and juicing good, he added, "Red Bolton figgers he's the cock of the dungheap hereabouts, and he don't brook no defiance."

When Skye entered the livery minutes earlier, Danny Ford had been seated on an old nail keg, trimming a horse's hooves with a hasp. But now he was busy hitching a big blood bay to a calash, a light, low-wheeled carriage with a folding top. Fargo had just rented it with more railroad money.

"Owen will soon be free," Fargo promised, patting the document Dusty had signed. "First I'm going to escort Danny and Miss Robinson until they're safely on their way. Then I'll visit Red Bolton again."

Slappy shook his grizzled head, frowning. "Young feller, I like you. You're all grit and a yard wide. But you're stark, staring crazy if you hang around these parts. That vigilante bunch has been lathering their horses hard lately. Ask me, they been tryin' mighty hard to catch somebody—*you*. And when they do, they mean to put a load of blue whistlers in your belly."

"That rings right," Fargo agreed cheerfully. "But don't forget—not until they get that gold."

After leaving Dusty to pack her things, he had paid fifteen cents for a hot bath at the Drover's Cottage. Then Fargo had quickly reprovisioned; grain for the Ovaro, some jerked beef and hardtack for himself.

"Mebbe they won't kill you right off," Slappy allowed. "But a few of Bolton's scum buckets have taken to carrying the Sharps Big Fifty, a long-range gun. Now ain't that uncommon queer if they don't mean to kill?"

"Slappy," Skye replied, checking his cinches and latigos as he finished rigging the Ovaro, "I'd like to jaw a little more. But me and Danny got a lady to pick up."

"Mr. Fargo?" Danny piped up, holding aloft a paper sack. "Couldja maybe get this to the kids?"

"What is it, son?"

"Horehound and peppermint candies. I bought 'em myself at Hobson's Mercantile. I just wanted to do somethin' for them poor kids."

Skye grinned, taking the sack and tucking it into a pannier. "I'll have to wait, Danny, until it's safe for them to have it. Else the Danford gang will know something's up. But you *are* helping them kids, and helping me and Dusty Robinson, too. I'll tell you flat out—the Trailsman says that Danny Ford is a good man to ride the canyons with. Now let's raise dust, pard."

The kid swelled up with pride before leaping into the calash. "Yessir!"

Fargo noticed, as he led the Ovaro out into the rutted and muddy main street, that Red Bolton's big claybank was still hitched out front of the stone-and-timber jail house.

"Watch your top-knots, boys!" Slappy hollered from inside. "Lead *will* fly!"

Slappy Hupenbecker's dire prediction did not come true, and Fargo got Danny and Dusty safely on their way to Fort Laramie.

He soon found out why when he returned to Bear Creek. Several newspaper reporters had shown up, for the orphan train crisis was galvanizing national attention. Obviously, Bolton had reluctantly called off his dogs, worried what the reporters might learn.

That also explained why Bolton offered only sullen, token resistance when Fargo showed up to free Owen Maitland. Bolton hardly looked at the statement Dusty had signed.

"I guess she musta got confused in all the excitement," he finally mumbled, tossing the key ring to Fargo. "Get the little barber's clerk outta here."

Five minutes later Fargo and Maitland were matching shots of Old Taylor bourbon at the Last Alibi. Both men sat with their backs to the wall, and Fargo had loosened his Colt in its holster.

"You all right, Owen?" Fargo inquired, studying the man's bruises and a swelling over his left temple.

"Thanks to you and Dusty I'm alive. I require some barbering, is all. And a tall glass of buttermilk soon's I get home, to settle my stomach. That jailhouse food ain't fit for a goat's belly."

"Well, I want to know everything you've learned," Fargo said. "But first I want you to promise me from now on, butt out and lay low. Stay home, lock your doors, and sleep on a gun. You've done your job. I promise, things will be coming to a head around here real quick."

Maitland nodded. "You got my word. All this cutting up rough is not my game, Skye. Hell, my rheumatism is giving me the devil after just one night in jail. But I heard plenty, all right. You were right. They're all thick as thieves, Danford's gang and Bolton's bunch. But Bolton, at least, is starting to panic as the story builds up in the newspapers. Slade Pendergast, the territorial governor, also happens to be an attorney who peddles the law and order line. He's never been overly fond of Red Bolton nor his vigilance committee."

Fargo nodded. "Yeah, behind all his bluff and bluster, Bolton acts like a man who's starting to get snow in his boots."

"Sure, and with these news hawks in town he knows he has to put on a show. He claims all his men are riding patrols simply to back your hand if any of the gang slip past you. In fact, it's *you* they're looking to nab, and I heard Bolton himself say they'd flay your soles if you don't talk. Desperate men are dangerous. Their big priority now is to capture you, then torture the location of that gold out of you."

"I figured that out already," Fargo assured him. "That's

why that dry-gulcher didn't try to kill me right off earlier today. It's probably the only reason they didn't kill you, too, just in case you might know where the gold is."

"So what's your next play, Skye?"

Fargo tossed back the last of his bourbon, then stuck his hat on his head. "Somehow, Danford is communicating with his cousin without coming down the face of that bluff. There's got to be some back way in. I'm going to sniff it out if I can."

By now the two men had stepped out onto the boardwalk.

"Well, you just watch yourself," Maitland advised. "It's got to be mighty rough out there."

Fargo nodded. But he told himself, as he glanced carefully around the ramshackle settlement of Bear Creek, rough was part of the attraction, to a truly free man. But how could he explain such feelings to men like Owen, men who depended on stores for their food and clothing? Owen was a good, likable gent. All too soon, however, these civilized townies would destroy the old frontier. Hell, already there were hardly any buffalo left south of the Republican River in Kansas.

But right now was no time for nostalgia about the past. Maitland returned to his rented room and Fargo stopped by the livery for his Ovaro. The pinto was well rested and fresh grained. Fargo headed due north toward the Middle Fork and Cheyenne creeks, opening his mount up to a steady lope.

This time, however, he avoided the bluffs beyond the creek, swinging wide to the west. He circled around behind the bluffs and began a methodical scouting pattern. Before he actually searched for that secret way out, he wanted to make sure the area was clear of Bolton's men. There were no reporters, way out here, to witness anything.

The only possible trouble Fargo spotted turned out to be a branding camp set up by rustlers. But he figured it was none of his mix. He had his hands full as it was. Besides, the line between a stray cow and a free-range maverick could stretch pretty thin sometimes. Especially since many rustlers were actually former homesteaders driven off their claims by greedy cattle barons.

Taking advantage of any ground cover he could find,

Fargo made his way back toward the north, or back side, of the bluffs overlooking Cheyenne Creek. It appeared to be a solid, sheer wall of limestone cliffs.

He moved in close and began a thorough search for openings. Fargo was working his way between two huge boulders, intending to search behind them, when he first noticed it—a steady, ominous, ticking sound. It took him a few moments to recollect the noise. It was being made by tiny, wood-burrowing insects known as death-watch beetles. According to the old legends, they were always heard just before a man met his death.

That thought made a bead of sweat zigzag out from his hairline and trickle down his forehead. But Fargo knew he had to press on, and quick. There were six helpless kids and a woman counting on him, and the desperadoes holding them might kill them all at any time.

Fargo squeezed his way into the narrow opening, his arms pinned close to his sides. He had just poked his head around one of the boulders when he came face-to-face with a set of small, dull eyes and a triumphant grin full of broken yellow teeth.

"*Got* you, you son of a bitch!" Nash Johnson crowed, even as he swung his Volcanic rifle by the barrel.

Fargo barely had time to flinch before the solid wooden stock crashed into his skull, and his world closed down to pain, then darkness.

8

Skye Fargo felt as if he were submerged in a deep, murky pool. Slowly he was rising toward the surface, where he could see a weak shimmer of light. But the closer he got to the light, the more it felt as if his head had just been mule-kicked.

His eyes eased open. The first thing he saw was the single eye of a rifle staring back at him. Fargo's head throbbed like a Pawnee war drum.

"Mister, looks like you got your tail in a crack," Nash Johnson greeted him, speaking with a hillman's twang. "Get up, and start marching. You found what you was lookin' for. But only a fool goes lookin' for his own grave."

Johnson wagged his Volcanic lever-action repeater for emphasis. Slowly, pain exploding in his head with each movement, Fargo rose to his feet.

His Colt was already tucked behind Johnson's bright red sash. But his captor hadn't noticed the Arkansas Toothpick in Fargo's boot. Unfortunately, Fargo was not in good fighting fettle. His vision was blurred, and his legs threatened to fold under him.

"Let's go, Fargo, get a wiggle on!" Johnson snapped. He pushed Fargo hard in the direction of an opening in the limestone wall. It had been conveniently hidden by the boulders in front of it.

Fargo led, Johnson ten feet behind him with his rifle at the ready. Fargo was forced to duck a little to keep from scraping his head on the rock ceiling of the winding tunnel. Kerosene lanterns had been strategically placed so that an eerie, flickering illumination kept the tunnel from total darkness. They wound their way steadily upward. Fargo had the unpleasant impression that he was trapped in the bowels of hell.

"Iffen you're feelin' froggy, mister, you just go ahead and jump," Johnson said behind him. "But I got my trigger sear filed down to a twitch. You try a fox play on me, I'll blow your gizzard out, I guarangoddamntee it."

About fifteen minutes later, the tunnel abruptly ended. Johnson called out, "Dakota! You in there?"

A muffled voice answered. "Yeah! What's on the spit, Nash? I thought you was on your way to Bear Creek?"

"I got him, boss! I got Fargo!"

"Great jumpin' Judas! Good work, Nash! Herd him on in."

The muzzle of the Volcanic jabbed him in a kidney. Fargo squeezed through a narrow cleft and suddenly emerged into a spacious cavern. A thickset, powerfully built man stood in the middle, leveling a Smith & Wesson magazine pistol on him. Dakota Danford wore a sneer of cold command.

"Well now—the great Trailsman," Danford greeted him. "A living legend don't look half so big when you got him close up."

Danford glanced at Nash. "Go fetch Booth," he ordered. "Tell Heck to bring Fargo's horse topside. Then have him stay on guard duty just in case this is a diversion plan."

Fargo glanced quickly around, taking in all the straw pallets and stacks of provisions. A fever-flushed little girl, no more than six or seven years old, lay on one of the crude beds. Despite his own danger, Fargo felt a pang behind his heart at the sight of the helpless little creature. Clearly she needed a doctor.

Beyond the wide cave entrance he could see Kristen McKenna seated in the grass, ringed by the rest of the children. Bright sunshine blazed a soft halo around her blond hair, and the bottomless sky behind her looked pure as blue china. She was reading something to the kids from a book. Evidently she didn't realize yet what was happening inside.

"Now, Mr. Fargo," Danford gloated, keeping the pistol aimed center of mass on his newest prisoner. "Let's me and you make medicine. You want them kids, and I want that gold."

73

Fargo, still wobbly in the legs, nodded toward the sick child. "That little girl needs a doctor."

"Them in hell need ice water, too! Never mind that brat, Fargo. Where's the gold? I'll knock your pie biters right out of your mouth if you don't start talking."

"You made a stupid play when you snatched those kids," Fargo replied calmly. "Folks from Boston to San Francisco are howling for your hide. Your best chance now is to give up your plan and rabbit while you can. The longer you let this thing fester, the deeper you dig yourself into a hole."

"Never mind the stump sermons, preacher. *I'm* the he-bear around here. Now where's that gold?"

Nash Johnson returned to the cave. He was accompanied by the same man Fargo had first seen two days earlier, the unkempt hard case with the cauliflower ear and the .38 pistol tied low, gunfighter fashion.

Booth Collins wore an expression of loutish cunning on his face. "Well, lookit here, chappies! The big hero himself, champion of the titty-babies."

"Nash," Danford ordered, "tie his wrists behind him tight. Then take him outside and lash him to that aspen tree near the entrance. When I get done with this bearded buckaroo, he'll be singing like a choir on Sunday."

Both Danford and Collins held their guns on Fargo as Nash followed orders. The color ebbed from Kristen's fall-apple cheeks when the prisoner was herded outside. But she remained cool headed and gave no sign that she recognized him.

"Inside the cave, children," she ordered, suspecting what was about to happen.

When Fargo was securely lashed to the tree, Danford slid a lethally honed bowie knife from the sheath on his belt.

"All right, big man, I'll just lay it on the barrelhead. Either you tell me where you hid them shiners, or I'll cut you into so many pieces they'll need a rake to bury you."

Fargo managed a nervy little grin. "And of course, once I tell you, then all my troubles are over, huh? Danford, you're a bigger fool than God made you. There's only one reason I'm still alive—the fact you don't know where that gold is and I do. I aim to keep things that way."

Danford's face grew purple with rage. His right foot flew

up, kicking Fargo hard in the crotch. This was followed by several hard, back-handed slaps that left Fargo's ears ringing.

"You pig-headed son of a bitch!" Danford growled. "Talk out, Fargo, or all three of us will take turns beating you until hell won't have it again!"

Danford had split both Fargo's lips, and he could taste salty blood. The combination of sweat and blood had drawn gnats, and now they swarmed in his eyes. The kick to his crotch had taken his breath away, and he was slow to reply.

"Danford, is it true you were born over in Hawk Springs?"

Danford's deep-set eyes narrowed in puzzlement. "Yeah, what of it?"

"Well I'll be damned," Fargo said. "I was told a snake never travels more 'n a mile from where it hatched. 'Pears I was misinformed."

This was so brazen and unexpected that Nash Johnson actually laughed with some admiration at Fargo's defiant courage. Even Booth Collins gave a grudging grin. But Danford scowled darkly and suddenly pressed the deadly edge of the bowie against Fargo's windpipe.

"Fargo, I'm warning you. *Don't* push me. I'm on the feather edge of cutting you open from neck to nuts. Either you tell me where that gold is, or you better be at peace with your maker."

"As to that, it don't really matter," Fargo replied with difficulty, for the blade pressed hard. "Rumor has it that heaven doesn't want me and hell's afraid I'll take over."

Again Nash Johnson chortled, impressed by the Trailsman's grit. "He ain't milk-livered, you gotta give him that, boys."

Booth Collins pressed in closer. "Ahh, he's plenty scairt, Nash, he's just whistling past the graveyard, is all. Now, the Apaches, they're partial to hanging a prisoner upside down over a small fire. They slowly roast his skull until the brains bubble. You want I should build a fire, boss?"

Danford, still pressing his knife to Fargo's throat, considered Booth's suggestion.

"Not a bad idea," he agreed. "But it takes too long."

"Then let's just run a picket pin through his balls," Collins said. "I done that to a U.S. marshal back in Abilene. 'Course, it eventually killed him, but I found out what I needed to know."

"Or I got my drinking jewelry," Johnson suggested. He pulled out a pair of crude iron knuckles made from horse-shoe nails welded together. "Slug him with these a few times."

Dakota shook his head. "Nah. I just remembered something. There's a, whatchacallit, an Achilles tendon just above the heel bone. Connects the foot to the calf muscle. It can't heal once it's severed. A man gets sliced deep there, he's a cripple for life. What happens to a trailsman then?"

Booth Collins grinned approval. "*That's* the gait! Hell, we don't even gotta bother pulling his boots off to cripple him. There's another one a them tendon thing-a-ma-bobs just inside each elbow, too. Two deep slices is all Dakota's gotta make, Fargo, and you'll hafta hire you some old squaw to hold your pizzle while you piss."

Danford moved his knife to Fargo's left side, then snugged it up tight into the crook of the elbow. With his wrists bound tight, and himself lashed securely to the tree, Fargo could do nothing about it but await his fate.

"Talk out, damn you!" Danford ordered. "Elsewise I'll do it, and mister, it ain't bluff. First the left arm, then the right. If that still don't do it, I'll get to carving on your heels, too."

Fargo's face mirrored nothing. But he felt the corroded pennies taste of fear in his mouth. Death, for a frontier drifter like him, had become as familiar as a man beside him. All men eventually died, and Fargo had learned not to fear the inevitable.

But being crippled for life—for a strong man who depended on his health and strength to survive, nothing could be a greater nightmare. It would be like clipping the wings of an eagle and leaving it to die on the ground.

Fargo's mouth formed a grim, determined slit. "You do that to me, Danford, you might as well just go ahead and kill me, because I'll never tell you where that gold is. Why should I?"

"All right, damn you! It's your choice. Say good-bye to your reputation, big man. Your wandering days are over. You're about to become a compost heap."

76

Danford flexed his arm, preparing to make the deep, sawing cut that would render Fargo's arm useless for life.

"Stop it, you fiend-begotten wretch!"

Kristen, her pretty oval face a mask of fear, had been watching from the cave entrance. Now she attacked Danford in a rush as unexpected as a whirling dervish. Laughing, Booth Collins grabbed her and pinioned her arms to her side.

Kristen aimed an entreating gaze at the prisoner. "Please, Mr. Fargo, tell them where the gold is."

"I'll do it, miss," Fargo replied, "if they let you and the young'uns go first. Otherwise, they'll just kill all of us once they've got the gold. They know they're going to hang, anyway, for killing those train crewmen."

Danford had already secretly concluded that no amount of torture or maiming could break this defiant man. Like a stoic Indian brave covered with coup feathers, he refused to give his captors that satisfaction. But the sudden interference by Kristen McKenna had given Danford an idea.

"T'hell with all this," he muttered. "Boys, I'll be right back."

Danford ducked into the cave. When he reemerged, he carried the ill Mattie in his arms. Fear was starched into her young face. Kristen cried out hysterically when Danford stomped right over to the lip of the bluff and dangled the little girl out over thin air.

"All right, Fargo, it's time to hold or fold. You got ten seconds to tell us where that gold is. If you refuse, I'm tossing this little girl off. After she lands on them rocks below, she'll be nothing but paste. Them's the hard-cash facts, mister. Now it's your call."

Fargo had expected something like this moment to arrive, and he had been forming a desperate plan. Now it was time to throw the dogs a bone.

"You win, Danford," he surrendered. "But I can't tell you where the gold is, not so's you could find it on your own. I'll have to take you to it."

A triumphant grin split Danford's big, bluff face. "Now you're talking sense, Fargo. Nash, cut him loose from that tree, then you and Booth go saddle our horses. Fargo, I'm warning you right now—if this is a trick, I'll personally throat-slash all six of them kids *and* the woman right before your eyes."

The gang kept their horses in a copse beyond the entrance to the cave. Fargo gave a slight sigh of relief when he saw his Ovaro among the four mounts Nash and Collins led back to the cave. The plan Fargo had been mulling was a long shot, but without the Ovaro it would be impossible.

"Heck," Dakota ordered as he swung his big bulk into the saddle, "you stay here with the woman and the brats. She knows by now we got an escape tunnel, so keep a close eye on 'em."

Heck Munro nodded. "That's fine by me, boss. This bastard"—he pointed his chin toward Fargo—"gives me the fidgets. You watch him close."

Booth Collins laughed. He sat astride his big seventeen-hand sorrel. "Don't you fret, Heck. It's easier to put socks on a rooster than to give Booth Collins the slip. I got me a reputation as a giant killer. And what I can't do with a short iron, Nash here can do with his rifle. Mister Skye Fargo has finally reached the end of his tether."

"Grab leather," Danford ordered Fargo.

Fargo made quick note of the fact that Johnson had removed the Henry rifle from Fargo's saddle scabbard. It was lashed behind Johnson's cantle.

"At least cut my wrists free so I can ride," Fargo complained. "Or do you figure you three armed and tough giant killers can't handle one man who's unarmed?"

"You priddy near *was* unarmed," Danford reminded him. "And you may be yet, you try and cross us. Cut his wrists loose, Heck. That's a fast-lookin' horse, Fargo. But just remember it can't outrun a bullet."

There was a slight delay, on the trail down, as the riders edged past the packhorse Johnson had killed. The ripening corpse had already been pulled aside just enough to clear the trail for one rider at a time. During all this, Booth Collins kept his .38 at full cock and aimed at Fargo.

When they reached the flat tableland below, Danford aimed a steel-eyed stare at their prisoner. "Which way, Fargo?"

This was the first tricky part, and Fargo kept his weathered face impassive. In truth, that gold was hardly more than a stone's throw away, buried in the nearby stand of trees.

But Fargo's habit of always throwing a wide loop when he scouted terrain had reminded him of the one spot where he just might, with luck and divine favor, make his escape. However, it wouldn't be an easy sell to these desperate and suspicious hardcases.

"That way," Fargo replied, pointing northwest toward the foothills of the Laramie Mountains. "I took it up into the high country and buried it near a logging flume."

"Logging flume?" Danford repeated. "You talking about Pete Henderson's timber operation? Why, Katy Christ! That's a hard three-hour ride from here."

"It's lying rubbish," Collins chimed in. "Why would he haul it that far, and so high up? Hell, he had no packhorse."

"This stallion of mine could chin the moon with an anvil on his back," Fargo replied. "You asked where I hid the gold, I told you. Did you expect me to bury it close by so's you'd find it easy? If you don't believe me, that's your lookout."

"All right," Danford decided. "We'll play it your way for now, Fargo. But you try to hornswaggle us, you're going to die hard, and that's a pure-dee promise."

Without further parley the four riders pointed their bridles northwest, Fargo hemmed in tight by Nash Johnson and Booth Collins. They kicked their mounts up to a steady lope and headed up toward the high rimland. Within two hours they had reached the first slopes of the Laramie range, ablaze with wild lavender. A few bald peaks of granite loomed high above the treeline.

"We close yet, Fargo?" Danford demanded, breaking the long silence.

"Pretty close," Fargo affirmed. "Not too far past that talus slide up ahead."

The spot Fargo had in mind had started out as a millrace, a man-made canal through which water flowed to run a mill wheel. But the old gristmill had been burned out years earlier in an Indian attack. Later, timber cutters had moved in, and the millrace had been turned into a flume, a steeply inclined chute for transporting cut logs down the mountain side to a sawmill far below. The lumber men were still well above them, out of sight and working the treeline.

Fargo could hear the water brawling and churning as the four riders moved carefully over the loose talus, their hoofclops echoing off the surrounding rock. They crested a low ridge, and now the flume was in sight below them. It was running fast and hard, swollen with spring snowmelt.

"All right, damnit," Danford said. "Where's that gold, Fargo? I ain't asking you again."

"We're practically standing on it."

"Well then, trot it out."

All four men swung down, Collins untying a shovel lashed to his saddle. Fargo bent as if hobbling the Ovaro, but left the rawhide hobble untied.

Fargo edged closer to the frothing water, watching out of the tail of his eye for the next log to come sailing down from above them. What he had in mind would require split-second timing as well as several fast, complicated moves. And he would have only one chance.

"It's under that," he said, pointing toward a slab of shale rock. "Buried down a few feet."

Grunting hard, Danford turned over the slab. The ground was pressed flat and crawling with slugs.

"That dirt ain't been disturbed," Danford said, aiming an accusing stare at Fargo. "What the hell you trying to pull?"

Collins thumbed his hammer back to full cock. Abruptly, Fargo spotted a huge log speeding down the flume, perhaps ten seconds above them.

"Here, I'll show you," he offered, snatching the shovel from Collins's left hand.

Fargo knew that Booth Collins was the main threat right now. So before any of the men could react to his grabbing the shovel, he swung the tool hard and beaned Collins in the skull with the blade, knocking him down. His next move was to snatch his Colt from behind Nash Johnson's sash, then jerk his Henry loose from Johnson's saddle lashings.

"Damn you, Fargo!" Danford swore, snatching at the flap on his holster.

Fargo had no intention of shooting it out. If he got himself killed now, Kristen and those kids were as good as dead. Even as he rammed the Henry into his own saddle scabbard, Fargo was already leaping toward the frothing lumber chute. While still in midair he gave a high, piercing whistle, a signal to the Ovaro to follow his master.

Fargo's timing wasn't perfect, but he managed to gain a purchase on that log as it shot past. Desperately hoping he wouldn't get his brains dashed out on the wild ride down, Fargo wrapped his arms and legs tight around his makeshift boat.

"Put at him!" Danford shouted behind him, and above the water roar in his ears Fargo heard a hammering racket of gunfire.

A hail of lead chunked into the log and whiffed past Fargo's head. He had no control over the rolling and tumbling of the log, and it kept spinning, putting him first underwater, then rolling him back up into clear view of the shooters.

During one fast roll, he glimpsed the stalwart Ovaro, dutifully crashing down the mountain slope, following the flume and his master.

"Drop his horse, Nash!" Danford shouted, his voice fading.

Fargo glimpsed Johnson drawing a bead on the Ovaro. Desperately clinging to the log with only his legs and left arm, Fargo drew his Colt and tossed a few snap-shots at Johnson. He couldn't even come close to aiming, not while bobbing and tossing like a cork on a stormy sea. But his shots were close enough that Johnson nervously covered down.

The flume was fast-moving, and elation swelled within the Trailsman as it began to appear as if he just might have pulled off a remarkable and hair-raising escape. Then, before he spun under the churning surface yet again, he saw Booth Collins back on his feet, blood pouring from a head wound, his .38 to hand.

He's a trick shooter, Skye reminded himself, but nobody is *that* good. He was already out of effective pistol range, and Collins had to be off-kilter after that shovel slap, no way he—

"Unh!"

Fargo grunted hard as white-hot pain lanced deep into his left calf, the bullet numbing his entire leg up to the hip. For a second he almost lost his grip on the log. Then, mercifully, the flume took a swooping turn, and Danford's gang lost their line of fire.

But it was still a long ride down, and Fargo was weakened by both his leg wound and the head blow Nash Johnson had dealt him earlier. Besides, the most treacherous stretch of flume lay ahead, and even if he made it down in one piece, he still had to outrun three enraged, gold-starved killers.

Grimly, his throbbing wound dealing him misery, Fargo literally hung on for dear life.

9

So long as he clung tight to the log, Skye Fargo rode the flume without serious difficulty. But near the bottom of the mountain side, the shallow trough gave way to a more deeply dug canal. This last part of the drop down turned into a churning, frothing torrent that bisected a wild gorge.

Logs weighing many hundreds of pounds spun crazily like twigs in a tornado. Fargo, tossed and buffeted like so much driftwood, expected to be crushed at any moment if one of them crashed into him. But then, in a matter of thirty wild seconds, the log he was riding debouched into a calm, still pool of water. He slowed almost to a stop. He was shot up a mite but grateful to be in one piece.

A sawmill was visible on the far shore about a thousand yards away. Fargo could see men stripping the bark off of logs with adzes, hear the screaming of the steam saw as it cut the logs into new lumber. He glanced quickly around, and then grinned when he spotted his ever-reliable Ovaro, calmly taking off the grass from the shore just behind him.

Fargo started dog-paddling toward shore, his wounded left leg sore and throbbing, but not so hot and numb now. Optimistic by nature, he considered himself damn lucky overall. He had successfully bluffed, then eluded, three stone-hearted killers without surrendering the gold. He was reunited with his horse, and even in possession of all three of his weapons, although his Colt and gunbelt ammo would need drying in the hot sun.

Just as important: Thanks to that wild, death-defying ride just now, he had a good head start on the Danford bunch. Their mounts could never negotiate the slope as the sure-footed Ovaro had, meaning they would have to take the much longer trail. That would give him time to tend to his wound and still get away while they were making the long ride back down the slope.

Fargo limped ashore, dripping wet, and the stallion bumped its nose into his chest in greeting.

"Timely met, old campaigner," Fargo said, quickly checking the pinto for wounds. "Leastways *you* ducked the bullets."

Wincing, Fargo sat cross-legged in the lush grass, sliding his buckskin trousers up to examine his wound. There was an angry, puckered mound of swollen red flesh where the bullet had entered the meaty portion of his left calf muscle. Because it had missed any veins or arteries, and lodged in hard muscle, there was plenty of pain but very little bleeding. Unfortunately, that bullet would have to be dug out, and the wound cauterized before infection set in.

"Might as well get 'er done," he muttered to himself, sliding the Arkansas Toothpick from his boot. "Time's pushing."

The moment Fargo first started gingerly probing the wound to locate the slug, his leg flared with hot pain, even some of Slappy's cheap wagon-yard whiskey would have been welcome right now. Biting down on the bridle reins, Fargo dug the slug out, hissing through clenched teeth at the razor-edged pain.

But removing the slug wasn't the worst part. Now the wound had to be cauterized to seal it against infection and prolonged bleeding. Yet, there was no time to waste building a fire or heating his knife blade until it glowed red-hot.

It would have to be done another, much faster, and even more painful, way.

Fargo stood up and dug through a saddle pannier until he found a few of the new-fangled phosphors wrapped in oilskin along with his flint and steel. Then he opened the loading gate on his Colt and shook one of the remaining cartridges out into his palm. It looked dry. Using his rock-solid molars like pliers, he carefully pried the lead slug loose from the brass cartridge.

Very carefully, yet working fast before the gunpowder got too damp from blood, he packed the 200-grain powder load directly into the wound. Then he scratched a phosphor to life with his thumb nail and touched it to the powder.

It ignited instantly, a shower of fizzling sparks, and the

smell of scorched flesh assailed Fargo's nostrils. For a few moments it felt like a hot branding iron was burning deep into his leg, and he couldn't hold back a little yelp of pain. But at least the wound was now sterilized, and the seared flesh had sealed at the edges, forming a natural bandage.

He folded his bandanna a few times and soaked it in water before tying off the wound to keep it from chafing. Then he held one hand out and measured four fingers between sun and horizon, determining about thirty minutes of daylight left.

No time to rest that leg, he told himself as he awkwardly swung up into leather and reined the Ovaro around to the southeast. He had to take advantage of this head start and get back to Devil's Catacombs before the gang did. He hated to ride after dark, for it increased the chances of laming his horse. But needs must when the devil drives. . . .

From here on out he had to keep the Danford bunch busier than a dog chasing four rabbits. Too busy protecting their own lives to threaten those of the captives. Fargo had learned it long ago, a lesson he lived by. It was the enemy aggressor who set the rules of combat. And when their rules included hurting innocent children, a man had to fight back with methods many would call brutal.

For brutes was exactly what he was up against. Lawless, pitiless monsters who could kill a child as casually as buttering a biscuit. So it had to be done tonight—a signal sent, a clear warning that went beyond verbal threats: *hurt even one of those kids, and I'll make you wish you'd died at birth.*

Fargo didn't send out the first soldier in this battle, *they* did. But when the blue haze of gunsmoke finally cleared, he was determined to be the last man standing.

He had seven good reasons for his determination, and they all had a name and a face, and no one else to protect them.

"Damnit, shut *up*!" Heck Munro snapped, his voice shrill with nervous tension. "I've had all I can stomach of that damned screeching and caterwauling. Next thing, you'll be breaking out a fiddle."

Munro stood just outside the cave entrance, his slouching frame backlit by the setting sun. Kristen watched him constantly pacing, edgy as a caged tiger. And he kept nervously checking and rechecking the loads in his Colt Model 1855 revolving-cylinder rifle. He had seen something below, coming from the direction of Bear Creek, that he definitely did not like.

"We're just having a sing-along to pass the time," she replied. "Surely you can't begrudge the children a simple bit of diversion, under the present circumstances?"

"Don't you buck me, woman! If there's one thing I don't hardly need right now, it's all that damn racket. A man can't hear himself think."

For the past hour or so Kristen had led the kids in singing popular tunes such as "Susan James" and "Little Brown Jug" and "The Man on the Flying Trapeze." But it couldn't take Kristen's mind off of her fear and concern for Skye. Was he even still alive?

Nor could she get her mind off little Mattie, who was now delirious with fever. Kristen was no doctor, but that poor, hapless child had the first stages of death stamped into her flushed features.

"Mr. Munro," she pleaded, "I appeal to your sense of humanity! If that sick little girl doesn't receive medical attention in the next twenty-four hours, she'll—"

Kristen stopped speaking, suddenly aware of how all the kids were watching her, listening, their faces fearful. Especially Sarah, Mattie's older sister.

"—she'll be in serious trouble," Kristen finished lamely.

"Dumplin', 'trouble' is now the street all of you live on," Munro replied, still watching something or someone down below on the tableland.

A cold feather of nervous fear tickled Kristen's spine. Was it a rescue party approaching? As badly as she wanted to get these kids to safety, she knew that none of them would survive if some well-intended, but ill-advised, posse tried to shoot their way up the bluff.

Given the complicated mess they were in, and the sick mind of Dakota Danford, only Skye Fargo and his lone-wolf methods could save the captives. Kristen was convinced of that. She hoped against hope that somehow he would outwit his captors and get away.

Taffy Mumford, seeing the worry lines on Kristen's pretty face, now spoke up.

"Ahh, we'll weather this," he said with bold assurance.

"We'll get out of this darn pukehole. And you know what? My mouth is watering for a good, thick venison steak."

"Me, I'm ready to wrap my teeth around some scrapple and eggs," Nick tossed in.

"No, hot flapjacks dripping with maple syrup," Liam insisted.

This got all the kids clamoring about what favorite food they most wanted to eat once they got free. So hope still lived within them. Gratefully, Kristen aimed a smile at Taffy. The fourteen-year-old winked at her, a saucy little wink that said: *Don't worry, gorgeous. This fight ain't over yet, so buck up.*

Just then, however, Mattie groaned pitifully in her feverish sleep. And Heck Munro, Kristen noticed, was now staring due south constantly in the fading daylight.

If you're still alive, Skye, she prayed silently, *please hurry.*

The moon was in full quarter, and an endless explosion of stars burned in a cloudless night sky, turning darkness into day. So Fargo knew that Danford's gang would almost surely try to cut trail on him in this clear light. Especially if they knew he was wounded.

At the first opportunity he deliberately rode across a sandy wash, making it appear that he had headed due east. Then, carefully backtracking across a rocky ridge, he again bore toward the Devil's Catacombs. Now and then he glanced up into the vast night sky, keeping the constellation Orion at his left for a reference point. His wounded leg was giving him grief. But it was good luck, his not having lost much blood—despite the burning pain, he felt alert and up to fighting fettle.

He was perhaps three miles north of Cheyenne Creek when the Ovaro's ears suddenly pricked forward. Fargo rode to the highest point nearby, then reined in. Wincing at the hard twinge of pain in his left calf, he stood up in the stirrups to see better. Spyglasses were useless after sunset, so he relied on his naked eyes.

Long years of scouting terrain had taught him the best use of his vision. He didn't try to focus on any particular spot in the vast, open vista before him. Instead, he simply let the entire landscape "come up to his eyes," looking for motion, not shape.

A straight-on look showed him nothing to worry about, so Fargo reined the Ovaro around a quarter turn and looked again from the corner of his eye. Sometimes peripheral vision detected movement that direct vision could not.

But still he observed nothing threatening with his eyes. Since sounds carried a great distance at night, he next relied on his frontier-honed hearing. He sat motionless for a full three minutes, simply listening.

In the near distance he heard a coyote yapping, a mournful sound. But soon enough a breeze stirred from the south, and Fargo detected a faint sound he recognized from his days as a contract scout for the cavalry—the clinking of harness and gear, the metallic rattle of bit chains.

It couldn't be Danford's bunch—they couldn't possibly be south of him. Nor would he be hearing it unless a large group of riders was out there somewhere. Fargo swung down and knelt, lightly placing his finger tips on the ground. His suspicion was confirmed when he felt the vibrating rhythm of approaching horses, which an experienced scout could detect many miles off.

"That's all we need," he muttered to the Ovaro as he gingerly stepped into leather again. "Crusaders whipped up by the newspaper scribblers. C'mon, boy, gee up!"

Fargo kicked the Ovaro up to a full gallop. He had feared something like this, and it only emphasized how urgent it was to get this rescue over with his way—and damn quick.

Knowing the riders must be headed toward the catacombs, he quartered around to the southeast, hoping he could intercept them in time. The Ovaro, sensing its master's urgency, lengthened its strides. They forded Cheyenne Creek in less than a minute, and by now the riders had loomed into view over the horizon line, dozens of them silhouetted against the blue-black night sky.

Fargo sat in his saddle on the south bank of the creek. This put him in plain view of the approaching riders, but hidden by trees from the bluffs behind him. The leader of the citizen's posse halted about twenty yards out, challenging him. Fargo had more rifles aimed at him than a target in a turkey shoot.

"Who are you, mister? Sing out quick, or you'll be pushing daisies!"

"The name's Skye Fargo," he replied calmly. "And you've no cause to threaten me."

"Fargo! Hell, you're the fella Peyton Norwood hired. I apologize, Mr. Fargo. We're just a mite edgy. The name's Stockwell, Ike Stockwell."

Stockwell nudged his big buckskin mare closer, the citizen's posse following him.

"We had you marked down for dead by now," Stockwell explained. He was a hawk-nosed, granite-jawed man in his early forties, wearing range clothes and a broad plainsman's hat. "Any word on them kids and the newspaper gal?"

"They're all still alive, and to speak plain, boys, I'd like to keep it that way."

"Well, hell! You think *we* come to kill 'em?"

Fargo forced himself to be patient. After all, these men meant well.

"Course not," he replied. "And if things stood different, I'd join you right now, Ike. But I think the best thing for the captives would be for all of you to dust your hocks back toward Bear Creek."

"You sound like Red Bolton. He threw a hissy fit 'bout us forming up a posse. All him and his jackleg deputies're doing is sittin' on their ampersands."

A cynical smile tugged at Fargo's lips. "Yeah, well, Red Bolton claims he's only obeying the railroad's request. But he's got private reasons for holding back. *My* reason is simple—the safety of those captives."

"Look, Fargo—Mr. Fargo, I mean. I know you got a reputation for knowing which way the wind sets, and I respect that. But I fought redskins, smallpox, and drought to build up my spread. And these lads backing me ain't townies, they're cowpokes and fur trappers and Injin fighters. We wasn't born in the woods to be scared by an owl."

"I don't doubt your mettle," Fargo said truthfully. "You gents ain't the problem. The thing of it is, your numbers won't matter. One sentry can pick you off at will as you charge up. Besides, this Dakota Danford ain't quite right in the head. Neither is the hired gun siding him, Booth Collins. You force their hand with a massed attack, they *will* kill those captives. I'll make you a deal. Give me forty-eight more hours to free them. If I can't get it done on my own, I'll join up with you boys."

Stockwell slowly rubbed his chin, thinking it over.

"Ike, I've heard of this Trailsman feller," spoke out a voice from the group of mounted men. "They say he's seen the elephant more than any ten men. But he works best when he's on his own, is what I hear. I vote let's try it his way. I got kids, too, and I don't want no dead young'uns on my conscience. And if I get killed tonight, my family will starve."

A few other voices murmured assent.

"All right, Mr. Fargo," Ike Stockwell finally said. "Since there's children involved, we'll stand down for two days. But after that, if you ain't got this Danford bunch hobbled, we're coming hell-bent for leather."

Fargo nodded. "Fair enough."

He waited until the riders had wheeled their mounts around and were headed south again. Then, sticking to the shadows cast by the same woods where he'd cached the gold, he forded the creek again. He quickly dug up the gold and counted out two hundred fifty double eagles—five thousand dollars worth.

Fargo figured he had at least an hour, maybe much longer, before Danford, Collins, and Johnson returned. That meant, once the posse turned back, Heck Munro would not be carefully guarding the trail up the bluffs—not with seven prisoners to keep an eye on.

Fargo had already considered the possibility of killing Munro while the rest of the gang were still gone. But no doubt he was sticking close to the captives, placing them in the way of any flying lead. Besides, there were no horses to get those kids out, and at least one of the youngsters was seriously ill. Also, with so many young ones they'd never get far on foot before the rest of the gang returned. And no doubt Red Bolton's men were out there patrolling somewhere. Fargo figured it was riskier to expose the kids in the open than to leave them where they were and take the risks himself. This way he had more control over the situation.

So he needed to see Kristen McKenna again and explain the strategy from here on out. It was going to get damn rough and ugly before things got better.

At the base of the trail, Fargo quickly dismounted and removed four pieces of square-cut rawhide from a pannier.

Using leather whangs, he tied one around each of the Ovaro's feet to muffle the ringing of horseshoes on rock.

Then, the butt-plate of his Henry resting on his left thigh, he started up the winding trail toward Devil's Catacombs.

"Well, God kiss me!" Heck Munro exclaimed. "The posse has turned back. You and them whelps just got mighty damn lucky, sugar britches."

Munro, obviously relieved, left the entrance of the cave and returned to the interior, spooning himself a plate of rabbit stew from the iron kettle kept warm over some embers. He had not seen a lone rider speaking to the men, only the fact that they had given up. He assumed Red Bolton had somehow averted the danger.

"Yessir, *mighty* damn lucky," he repeated, squatting on his heels to eat. He kept his rifle to hand and faced the cave entrance at all times. "I got my orders what to do if anybody rushes this place."

Kristen felt a flutter of nausea as she realized her guess had been right about a citizen's posse. She and the children had somehow just escaped a violent death.

"Now, Skye Fargo—*he* ain't so lucky," Munro added, wiping his greasy chin on his sleeve and chewing with his mouth open. "I figure by now Dakota's got that gold and Fargo is cold as a wagon wheel."

Kristen, her nerves stretched to the breaking point, slid a slim silver flask from her valise. It contained red wine, for she was not a tippler of hard spirits. Before she could even remove the stopper, however, she heard the sound from outside—an owl hoot.

Skye! Oh, dear lord, *please* let it be Skye's signal, she prayed.

"I'll be back soon," she remarked casually as she stood up, smoothing her skirt. "I need to bathe."

Munro laughed, revealing teeth like rows of crooked yellow gravestones. "Take your time, city princess. I know you ain't going nowhere without this brood. 'Sides, me and the boys will be wantin' you to smell real good . . . for later."

His obvious hint sent a chill of revulsion through her. "Taffy, you're in charge of the kids," she said before she left. He understood her meaning—yell out for her if Munro turned abusive.

Kristen, gathering up her skirts to avoid cockleburs, picked her way through the wooded bluff, heading toward the pond. What if that had just been a real owl? Skye could not possibly have escaped from—

A strong arm encircled her waist from behind, picking her right up off the ground, and a bearded face nuzzled the back of her neck.

"Skye! Oh, it *is* you! Oh, thank God! But how—?"

"Never mind, sweet love, it's a long story. I figure in about an hour or a little longer Danford and the others will be returning. And be prepared. He didn't get that gold, so he's going to be madder than a badger in a barrel."

"Oh, why won't he just give up and run? Can't he see the trouble he's in?"

"Dakota Danford," Fargo informed her, "is a one-trick pony. His mind is fixed on destroying the railroads. He might eventually decide to high-tail it, but not before he . . . does something to make the nation hate the railroad barons."

"You mean kill me and the kids," Kristen said frankly. "But why? How can one man be so consumed by hatred?"

"Some men are just spiteful and mean by nature. But it's not *just* his personal grudge that's behind all this. It's also the gold sickness. It's muddied up his thinking."

Fargo still vividly remembered the get-rich-quick fever of the Argonauts, the California gold seekers named after the legendary men who sought the Golden Fleece. Men killed their own brothers over claim disputes, deserted wives and children to go chasing after a dream of wealth.

They were finishing the walk toward the pond and its surrounding bed of pine needles.

"Skye?"

"Hmm?"

"Do you know what quinine is?" she asked.

"Medicine, isn't it?"

"Yes, it's a medicinal powder extracted from tree bark. It was developed for treating malaria, and it can work miracles in reducing dangerous fevers. Little Mattie Everett is only seven, and I'm certain she's going to die if I can't bring her fever under control."

"Yeah, I saw her, poor kid. How much time?" Fargo asked.

"If she doesn't receive a dose by sometime tomorrow,

with follow-up doses, I fear it will be too late. It works quickly. I can easily mix it in her drinking water so Danford's gang won't even know."

"If she needs it," Fargo said, "that settles it. There's a doctor in Bear Creek. Think he'll have some?"

"Yes, for it's too handy not to have and very inexpensive."

"I'll head to Bear Creek this very night. But I'll have to climb up the bluff next time, so listen for the owl hoot again." Fargo pointed. "And just in case you can't get out, I'll leave it under that dead log right there."

"Oh, thank you, Skye! It's her only chance. You—why, Skye, are you limping? What happened?"

"My leg got in the way of some lead. Nothing serious, I took care of it. Still stings a mite, is all."

"Here," she said, offering him her flask. "Sorry it's only wine, but maybe it will help the pain."

"Wine?" he teased her, ignoring the flask. "That's just vinegar sneaking up on old age."

She laughed, the first in some time.

"You know," she told him, "at first I saw you as an excellent example of the benighted savage on the wild frontier. But I was wrong—you are 'a gentleman unafraid.' "

"There's the flowery writer in you spouting off again," he said as he began to unbutton her dress.

"Oh, indeed, Mr. Fargo? Then let me 'spout off' about something else I've noticed concerning you. Something intriguing and different. You're an incredibly handsome man, but quite comfortable with your rugged good looks. I know handsome men in Manhattan, too. But their looks have gone to their heads."

Skye had her dress open now and was cupping the impressive heft of her breasts. His thumbs traced slow circles around her nipples, making them stiffen into hard bullets.

"The damndest things will come out of a woman's mouth," he replied.

"Well, then, why don't you just kiss it shut?"

He accepted the challenge, their tongues probing each other's hungry mouth like exploring fingers. Her hand snaked down inside the front of his tented trousers, stroking and squeezing his hard member until his loins heated up like a smithy's forge at full-bellows.

"You're playing with fire, girl," he moaned, his voice a lust-thickened husk.

"Then burn me!" She flung herself at him, so hot she was panting.

Despite her trembling fingers, she quickly stripped off her petticoats and cotton pantaloons while Fargo dropped his trousers, making sure his Henry was close to hand. He pulled her down onto their soft, pine-scented bed. She was quivering like a rain-soaked kitten, for right now all she wanted was to be taken out of herself, her horribly troubled mind set free of worrisome thoughts.

"You know what I like," she moaned, lifting her breasts toward him as if in offering. "Just like you did last time?"

Fargo took each stiff, spearmint-flavored nipple into his mouth, driving her to a shuddering ecstasy of pleasure. Meantime, he parted her shapely thighs and caressed the glazed, chamois-soft folds of her womanhood, stimulating her pearly nubbin until she climaxed so hard her body jack-knifed up off the ground.

"Now it's *your* turn," she whispered, straddling his chest backward and lowering her mouth over his hard, curving length. Her long hair, unpinned now, fanned out over his belly, softly tickling, and as she took him into her mouth Fargo groaned encouragement.

He cupped her firm round butt cheeks to steady her as her head began bobbing up and down, faster and faster, firing a thrumming pleasure in his groin. She flicked her tongue quickly around the purple-swollen dome of his manhood, lightly raked her teeth along the sensitive underside. Pleasure too intense to control made his entire body twitch. As her passion grew more intense, she took more and more of him into her mouth, so deep her tonsils tickled him. There was far too much of him to accommodate. So she gripped the rest of his length and stroked him fast and furiously.

Pleasure washed over the Trailsman in delirious waves, and he felt himself turning rock hard in her mouth as he held off as long as he could. Then, his hips bucking like a wild mustang fighting the halter, he spent himself in powerful, shuddering spasms.

The force of his climax left him lazy and drifting, so content he couldn't even feel the raw soreness in his wounded leg. For some time it was absolutely quiet except for a gentle whisper of breeze and the bit-champing of the Ovaro, tethered nearby.

But, by reluctant and long-established habit, he forced his mind back to the danger they faced. After all, they were not on holiday in New Orleans. He had to send his warning to the gang, then get back down that trail before the rest arrived. And there was still a long ride back to Bear Creek for that medicine.

They both began dressing while Fargo explained the strategy from here on out. Except for some details he hoped she would never know about.

"It's going to be a tricky piece of work," he admitted. "I've got to keep them scared to hurt you and the kids, but also stroke their greed for that gold. And I think I know how to do it, with your help. But you've got to understand, from here on out, it's going to get ugly now and then. Maybe damn ugly. Not by my choice, either. This thing has got to be done on my terms now, and done quick. Do you understand?"

She nodded, her face luminous and beautiful in the soft moonlight and the glow of their lovemaking. She buttoned her dress as if in a trance.

But then the import of his words sank in, and her face firmed up with determination.

"Yes," she said emphatically. "I trust you, Skye. They've forced your hand. And anything you do, from here on out, is for the sake of those kids."

"And you, pretty lady."

"Yes, and for me."

"All right," Fargo said, grabbing his Henry. "Now scoot back to the cave. And here's what I want you to do. . . ."

10

Heck Munro, busy building himself a smoke, looked up in surprise when Kristen McKenna came running into the cavern. Her soft-blue eyes were big and wide with fright.

"What the hell? You seen a ghost out there?" he demanded. "You was sure's hell gone long enough to meet one."

"A bear!" she exclaimed. "It almost got me."

"You don't say? Hell, that must be the same bear Booth heard the other night. Big son of a gun?"

"Not too big, I don't think."

"Then it ain't no grizz, at least. Was it brown or black?"

"Black, I think."

"Well now . . . a bearskin makes for good sleeping of a night. And the haunch meat makes a tasty stew."

Heck Munro was bored anyway. He set the makings aside, he could smoke later. A grizzly was death to the devil and best avoided at all times. And a full-grown brown bear, too, was large enough to pose trouble even when shot. But black bears rarely exceeded three hundred pounds and were easy to drop.

Munro rose to his feet, debating. Coming out of the well-lit cave, he didn't trust his night vision for aiming his rifle. So he picked up Dakota Danford's unloaded double-ten express gun leaning against the side of the cave, one of many items Danford had stolen from Overland while working for them as a division superintendent. Munro broke the scattergun open, slid two shells into the chambers, and shut the breech.

No need for close aiming now, just spray pellets in the

general direction. This little puppy, he told himself, would blow the side out of a mountain.

"Just sit tight," he ordered Kristen as he headed for the mouth of the cave. "That bear is about to cross the Great Divide."

Skye Fargo waited in the moonlit darkness to see if Heck Munro took the bait.

Fargo wasn't looking forward to what had to be done. But he had already decided to fight this battle Indian fashion because surprise tactics, and unconventional fighting, were the only way to save Kristen and those kids. He had to weigh the life of one murdering hard case against those of seven innocent victims. Looking at it that way, a man had to do whatever it took. Danford forced this situation by his despicable crime, and every one of his men was a willing partner in it.

Fargo had removed one of the rawhide muffles from the Ovaro. He then wrapped it around a fist-sized rock and looped it around his wrist—an Indian trick for killing without noise. Silence was essential. He wanted those kids absolutely ignorant about whatever happened out here. Both for their own peace of mind and so they wouldn't have to lie to Danford when he returned and demanded to know what happened.

Munro was suddenly silhouetted in the cave entrance, a double-barreled shotgun at the ready. Fargo, hiding among the bushes, tugged a rope he had tied to a tree limb twenty feet away.

The limb rattled, and Munro instantly whirled in that direction, pointing the shotgun.

"Come to papa," he called out, advancing farther out of the cave.

Again Fargo rattled the limb, this time even harder. He added a few woofing grunts.

"Oh, I'm gettin' a good bead on you, brother bear," Munro gloated, moving even closer. "Stir around some more."

Fargo didn't want him discharging that cannon and frightening the kids. He moved quickly and silently, placing each foot carefully to avoid ground noises. He hooked around behind Munro.

Fargo set his heels and swung the heavy rock hard, wanting to get it over quickly. Time was pressing in now. He had to ride down from here before Danford and the others returned. Munro gave one soft, surprised little grunt before he collapsed as if his bones had gelled.

Fargo felt for a pulse and found none. He had smashed Munro's skull in one blow. It was a clean kill done as mercifully as he could, given the circumstances.

"I didn't want it this way, mister," he muttered regretfully. "With me it's live and let live. But you forced it when you took those kids. May the Almighty have mercy on your soul."

Fargo swung the double-ten express gun hard into a tree, snapping the barrel from the walnut stock. Now he had to leave an unwritten but clear message for the rest of the gang. But Fargo also wanted to provide some incentive for them, a way of promising that humane behavior would be rewarded. So he dumped the gold double eagles all over the remains.

The twin message was crystal clear: Treat those captives right, and the gold may still come your way. Treat them wrong, and this is the fate awaiting you.

Limping slightly because of his throbbing leg wound, Fargo quickly returned to his pinto stallion. Danford's bunch would be returning any moment now. Fargo had to get down off the bluffs and make the long ride to Bear Creek in quest of medicine for little Mattie.

It had been a long, eventful day, and his eyelids were growing heavy. And his hungry belly gnawed at him. But sleeping and eating would have to wait—as would everything else until that medicine was delivered to Kristen.

"I thought we had Fargo certain-sure," Nash Johnson said for at least the third time since they'd left the Laramie Mountains.

Johnson's reedy twang was getting on Dakota Danford's nerves.

"Why'n't you set it to music?" he snapped. "Yeah, he foxed us this time. So what? I got my belly full of Skye Fargo. We *will* put the quietus on that son of a bitch, all in good time. I'm pretty sure Booth tagged him in the leg.

That's prob'ly why he took off to the east—he's hit too bad to keep fighting."

"Just hope he don't bleed out," Nash replied. "We'll never lay hands on that gold withouten we find Fargo agin."

Danford, Johnson, and Booth Collins were nearing the top of the only trail leading to the cave. Collins was in a sullen, silent mood. He had an ugly gash on his left cheek, a legacy of his collision with that shovel.

The weary trio rode their horses to the clearing behind the pond. The men were too tired and out of sorts to rub down their mounts and curry off the dried sweat. So they simply stripped off the saddles and bridles and put the horses on long tethers so they could drink and graze.

"Where's Heck?" Danford demanded the moment the three men entered the cave.

Kristen, busy reading a Charles Dickens novel to the children, glanced up.

"I believe he went outside to make a necessary trip," she replied.

" 'Necessary trip'!" Collins repeated, his voice tight with mean sarcasm. "Oh, don't *she* sneeze through silk?"

Collins, frustrated and angry, kicked at Taffy. But the streetwise city tough was too quick and ducked just in time.

"Like I told you, half-pint," Collins snarled. "You're *mine*. That cocky look will come off your face soon enough, sonny boy."

Collins slanted his hateful gaze toward Nick. "And you, peg-leg, the hell *you* staring at?"

"Nothing, mister," Nick shot back boldly. "Nothing at all."

"Why, you sawed-off, crippled-up little mutt, I'll—"

"Knock it off, Booth," Danford snapped. "Look at you, picking fights with brats barely out of three-cornered britches! I'm tired of hearing it. We got more immediate troubles."

He turned his deep-set, flinty eyes to Kristen. "How long ago did Heck leave?"

"I'm not really sure, I've been reading. I believe he also said something about shooting a bear. He took a shotgun with him."

Danford didn't like the sound of this. "I told him not to leave these captives alone too long," he told the other two men in a quiet voice. "Heck ain't too bright, but he's one to follow orders. How come he didn't sing out when we rode up? C'mon, let's take a look outside."

"Ahh, it's all right, I heard that bear, too," Collins said although he followed the others outside, his .38 to hand.

"Yo, Heck!" Danford roared in a bullhorn voice. "Heck! You out there?

"Fan out," he said quietly to the other two. "And keep your guard up. Something ain't quite jake here."

After a couple of minutes of quiet searching, Nash Johnson's shocked voice broke the stillness.

"Suffering Moses!"

This was followed by harsh retching sounds when Johnson vomited. The other two men ran over to join him. Silently, shock and revulsion starched into their features, they stared at Heck Munro's corpse and the place where his skull had been broken like an egg. He had died with his eyes open and seemed to stare back at them in the ghostly moonlight. Gold coins glowed like foxfire all over the body.

"Katy Christ," Danford finally swore when he could trust his voice. "Fargo led us on that wild-goose chase so he could do this. Had it planned all along, just like he did with the buried-gold trick."

Even Collins was so shocked the swagger had left his manner. "The Sioux and the Cheyenne sometimes kill with a head bash like that."

"It wasn't no redskin what left that gold," Danford reminded him, turning away in disgust. "That bastard's got more hard in him than I figured. Matter fact—"

Danford paused and sent a careful, nervous glance all around them. "We don't know for sure he ain't still up here, do we?"

Nash Johnson didn't need to hear a suggestion like that, not at the moment. He was afraid to even look at the corpse again. He came from hill folk who were mighty superstitious about the dead. It was said that spirits had twenty-four hours to hang around the spot where their body was killed, giving them a chance to possess another body. Hell, maybe Heck was taking over his body right this minute.

"Boss," he said in a quavering voice, glancing nervously all around them, "we're down to bedrock and showing damn little color. Maybe this thing's dragged on too long. Maybe it's time we cut our losses and—"

Danford's angry voice cut him off in midsentence. "And maybe you're a squaw man, Nash! You want color? Well, that air's *gold* piled on Heck. 'Zacly the color we want. We ain't pulling up stakes yet, you hear me? Fargo will bark in hell before he scares *me* off. First I aim to get more of this gold."

Squatting down, his face a twisted mask of rage and disgust, Danford carefully started picking gold coins off the dead man. Some were bloody and had to be wiped off in the grass.

"Don't you two see it?" he added. "Fargo is making us an offer—long as those captives live, that gold can still be ours. But he's also putting us on notice. Hurt those captives, and we die hard."

"Now, ain't *that* a case of the drizzlin' squitters?" Collins demanded. "T'hell with Fargo. Let's just kill one of them brats right now and—"

He never finished his thought. For a big man, Danford could move like lightning. He suddenly shot back up on his feet and grabbed the front of Collins's calfskin vest, twisting it so hard Collins could barely breathe.

"Damn you, Booth, I'm the ramrod here, y'unnerstan'? You will *not* hurt that woman or the brats, and that's an order! There's thousands of dollars right here in front of us, and more to be had if we play this right. Either us three stick together, or we'll all swing."

He turned Collins loose and looked at Johnson. "And Nash, act like you own a pair! This ain't no time to get icy feet. Fargo got lucky today, and he took this hand. But luck don't last a lifetime unless a man dies young. This thing ain't over by a long shot, boys. You wait and see—the worm *will* turn."

Fargo was feeling saddle-sleepy by the time the darkened town of Bear Creek loomed into view. He figured there was maybe two hours left until dawn. But, as usual, he assumed there were eyes watching him.

He swung down in front of the feed stable, regretting

that he would have to wake up Danny and Slappy. Fargo was reaching out to swing open the big side doors when he heard it, the menacing, tell-tale click of a rifle hammer being thumbed back.

He dropped flat into the hoof-packed dirt of the yard only a fractional second before gunfire erupted. Wood splintered where, a moment earlier, his head had been. Fargo shucked out his Colt and rolled a few times, coming up behind a stone watering trough.

He searched the shadows across the street, hoping to spot muzzle flash. But the shots had ceased. Moments later he heard feet running through the alley between Hobson's Mercantile and the Last Alibi saloon.

Fargo knew it was one of Bolton's toadies, and he also figured he could catch him if he gave chase. But he had come to town mainly to get the quinine, and he had to get it back up on the bluff as quickly as possible. Saving a sick little girl rated higher, to Skye Fargo, than ridding the world of one more back-shooting criminal.

At least he didn't have to worry about waking up the hostlers—the gunfire had done that for him.

"What in holy hell is all that racket out there?" Slappy's gravelly voice yelled out.

"It's just me, old timer," Fargo called back. "Bolton had a little reception committee for me."

"Skye Fargo, you son of trouble! I see Bolton and his scavenging curs ain't kilt you yet, by Godfrey! Hold on, boy!"

Fargo stayed behind the trough while Slappy, wearing only sagging red long-handles, lit a lantern and swung the doors open. Danny appeared behind him, his hair sleep-tousled.

Fargo grabbed the bridle reins and led the Ovaro inside. "Sorry for the fireworks, fellas, I know it's early. Danny, get to work on my horse, would you? A good rubdown and curry, then grain him. I got another long ride to make."

"You bet, Mr. Fargo. Got the rest of them kids yet?"

"I'm working on it, Danny," Fargo assured him.

"You see the puke pail that tried to plug you just now?" Slappy asked.

Fargo shook his head. "No, but this is an interesting development. Up to now Red Bolton was holding off on killing me—his cousin's orders, no doubt, until I turned over the gold. But this just now tells me that Bolton is starting to panic. His share of that gold no longer matters. He just wants to clear himself, and that means killing the one man who's promised to expose his part in the crime."

"Tell the truth and shame the devil," Slappy agreed. "Bolton knows damn good and well his cousin Dakota wouldn't piss in his ear if his brains was on fire. Now he just wants shut of the whole mess."

" 'Specially," chimed in Danny, busy drying the Ovaro with an old feed sack, "now he's got this new trouble with Dusty Robinson."

"What trouble?" Fargo demanded. "You did get her to Fort Laramie safely, didn't you?"

"Sure he did," Slappy said. "That boy's reliable as a Kentucky rifle. But Owen Maitland has got a good think piece on him. He slipped one a them—whatchacallit?—anonymous letters to one of them reporters in town. Them newspaper dandies is all filing 'wild West' stories while they wait out this business with the kids. So Owen told how Bolton tried to frame him for attempted rape. Governor Pendergast read it, and he's bilin' mad. Promised to investigate, and prosecute Bolton if there's evidence."

That tugged a grin out of the trail-weary Fargo. "So the plot thickins? Well, if the heat under Bolton gets too hot, I'm thinking he'll throw in with his cousin and try to run. When a rat panics, it seeks the safety of the pack."

Slappy pointed out the open doors with his chin. "Speaking of Bolton, yonder he comes now, and it looks like he's got sand in his ointment. I swear, ever time that man draws close, I smell a whiff of skunk."

Fargo put a wall to his back and rested his palm on the butt of his Colt. Bolton had two men siding him, both wearing big hog-leg pistols.

The three men stopped inside the doorway.

"I mighta knowed it was you behind all this ruckus, Fargo," Bolton greeted him. "I got a good mind to arrest you for disturbing the peace."

Fargo snorted. "You ever take time to smell what you're shoveling, Bolton? First you order one of your lick-spittles to throw lead at me, then try to toss *me* into the calaboose?"

"That's balderdash!"

Fargo goaded the phony lawman with a tight-lipped smile. "It's clear now that you're eager to get me out of the picture. But how do you plan to explain that to Peyton Norwood and the reporters for the crapsheets, not to mention Governor Pendergast? The noose is tightening for you, *sheriff*."

Bolton was indeed getting worried. Fargo watched sweat bead up under his hat brim. "You're crazy as a shite-poke, Fargo!"

Fargo didn't let up, turning the screws even tighter. "Yessir, Red, it's the gallows limb for you. Your big mistake was in trying to profit off your cousin's madness. Now he'll drag you down with him. Ain't nothing like that last snap when your neck breaks."

"Don't dance on my grave too quick, Fargo. It'll be a holiday in hell before you pin anything on me."

Fargo never once took his attention away from the two men siding Bolton. The dime novelists had it all wrong—Fargo had learned long ago to watch the hands, not the eyes. Eyes couldn't pull a trigger.

"So far I've planted one of your cousin's men, Bolton," Fargo said calmly. "And one of yours. The blooding has just begun. You can still save your worthless hide if you confess and turn yourself in. You might get off with a ten-year prison stretch."

"Stretch a cat's tail, you smug son of a bitch! C'mon, boys, let's clear out. I'm just a whisker away from killing that lanky bastard."

"Oh, we'll be huggin' again," Fargo promised before Bolton stomped off, his men in tow.

Slappy, busy uncorking his jug, chuckled with glee. "It's a reg'lar tonic, Skye, seeing ol' Red all tied up in conniption fits. Usually it's him what holds all the aces. But you best look sharp, boy. That peckerwood is scairt spitless, and a scairt man is a dangersome man. Care for a snort?"

Fargo took one burning swallow to cut the trail dust in his throat.

He handed the jug back to Slappy, who tipped it again. "I never stop at one or go past ten," he said, smacking his lips.

Then Slappy took a closer look at the Trailsman in the

flickering yellow lamplight. "Say! You best get some shut eye, young feller. You look plumb tuckered out."

"Can't, dad. I'm on a medical mission. There's a pill merchant in this town, right?"

"Sure, but ol' Doc McGillycuddy is a gruff old coot who don't cotton to late-night business. You might roust out Owen Maitland first. Him and Doc are good friends and poker buddies."

Fargo nodded, headed toward the door. "I need to check on Owen anyway. Danny, put a hustle on it, I'll be riding out directly. Check the hooves good for stones or cracks."

Something else occurred to Fargo, and he turned around again.

"Danny, can I count on you for more help?"

"You bet your bucket, Mr. Fargo! Just name it."

"Later on this morning I want you and Slappy to pick out a string of, say, five small horses, nothing bigger than fourteen hands. Gentle animals preferred. Have them ready to tack, and make sure the stirrups are adjusted high for a child. Then, later this afternoon, I want you to ride to Middle Fork Creek and wait for me. And bring the horses."

"Yessir! But only five horses? There's seven captives, ain't there?"

"The two smallest kids will need to double up with older ones. Now, Danny, promise me you will *not* ride north of Middle Fork?"

"Hand to God, Mr. Fargo."

Fargo nodded to the kid. "You're a great help to me and the kids, Danny. You and Slappy both."

Slappy, who'd become something of a cracker-barrel philosopher in his old age, watched Fargo disappear into the shadowed street.

"Right there goes the backbone of America, Danny boy," he opined. "And pond scum like Red Bolton just might be her epitaph, the no 'count son of a buck."

Owen Maitland rented a room on the ground floor of the Drover's Cottage, a hotel hardly bigger than a packing crate. Fargo, his eyes flicking to all sides, stuck to the shadows as he slipped around to the back door of the building.

Owen's room was midway down the hallway, a narrow corridor lighted by one lantern in a brass wall sconce. Fargo rapped softly and was surprised at the almost instant response.

"Friend or foe?"

"Skye Fargo, Owen. Sorry to disturb you."

A bolt shot, and the door swung open. Fargo got a quick glimpse of a room just like its tenant—clean, and neat as a pin. A surveyor's transit and other instruments were neatly stacked in one corner.

"Skye, am I glad to see you still among the living," Maitland greeted him. "Hurry on in before they ambush you again. I heard the shots a few minutes ago and figured the target might be you."

Owen was fully dressed except for shoes and wore a small gun in an armpit holster.

"I took your advice," he explained when he saw Fargo looking at the weapon. "It probably wouldn't help me. I can sight a Gunter's chain fine, but I don't even know how to aim a firearm. I doubt if I could hit a bull in the butt with a banjo. But I feel better having it."

"You don't bother aiming a pistol, Owen. It's only useful at close distances anyway, and the delay will just get you killed. Just pretend it's an extension of your finger. All you do is point at your target and shoot."

"I'll be dang sure to remember that. What brings you to town, besides a death wish?"

Fargo quickly explained the dilemma with little Mattie Everett.

"That poor child," Owen sympathized. "Don't worry, we'll roust out Doc McGillycuddy. He's hard of hearing, and he sleeps at the rear of his office. But I know where he hides the key in case of emergencies. Just let me put my shoes on."

Owen sat on the edge of the bed to button his shoes.

"I heard what you did," Fargo said. "Telling the newspapers about Bolton's attempted frame-up of you. It's got him skittish, too. Good work, old son."

Owen grinned. "Oh, his troubles have only started. Yesterday I sent a letter by special courier to Slade Pendergast, the territorial governor. I detailed everything. Pendergast is a former prosecutor from back east, a big law-and-order type who's eager to get rid of these vigilance committees and set up a court system with circuit judges and U.S. marshals. But we'll still need some proof besides hearsay. Dusty will testify against Bolton, but that's a minor crime compared to some of his capers."

"I got a hunch it won't end up in court," Fargo replied. "Bolton knows he's due for a reckoning. I expect him to rabbit any time now."

"Well, I'm all set," Owen announced, standing up. "Let's go get that medicine."

"You sure you want to appear on the street with me? Lead tends to fly in my area."

"Then let 'er rip," Owen said with heartfelt conviction. "Red Bolton and his minions have had this town paralyzed with fear for years now. Then a tall stranger with an even taller reputation rides in among us. A man willing to lay his life on the line for children he doesn't even know. If *you* are ready to die for the cause of justice, the rest of us need to pitch in, too."

Fargo had never been overly fond of townies. But he felt a surge of admiration for this slight, well-spoken man with a conscience as big as all Texas. Dusty Robinson had echoed similar sentiments. Thank God the West was populated with decent folks, too.

"I got a hunch," Fargo told him, "that this town has got a bright future. Now let's both quit slopping over and get that medicine. Time's a-wastin', and we got a little girl to keep among the living."

11

"Damnit, Dakota, we're just sitting ducks up here," Booth Collins complained hotly. "It was fine for a day or two. But now it's time to vamoose."

"I been studying on that," Danford said evasively.

"Well, don't 'study' too damn long, or all three of us will be wearing hemp neckties. Admit it, you been thinking the same thing. I notice you ain't crowing so much anymore about all them chilipep whores we're going to enjoy down in Old Mex."

Booth and Dakota were conferring near the back of the cave. Kristen, busy preparing cornmeal mush for the kids' breakfast, could overhear them if she listened close. Outside, the sun was newly risen and she could hear the dawn chorus of birds welcoming the new day. Some of the kids were awake and lying quietly on their pallets; a few still slept.

"Sure it's too dangerous to stay here much longer," Danford conceded. "Last report I got from Red, newspaper scribblers are flocking to Bear Creek. I knew this place was risky if things dragged on too long. And that's exactly what Fargo has managed to do—drag it out. But I planned on us being outta here within forty-eight hours or so. Long before it turned into a crusade in the newspapers."

"Well, you done a bang-up job of *that*," Collins retorted sarcastically. "Big man with big plans! I had me a nice deal on a rigged faro wheel in Saint Louis. Now here I am with my ass hanging in the wind."

Neither man took his eyes off that narrow, nearly hidden cleft that led to the rear tunnel. Nash Johnson was out front guarding the trail. Both approaches were watched constantly now. Kristen thanked the good Lord above for the fact that all three men still didn't realize Skye Fargo had found a third way up. They figured they were reasonably secure if they watched both approaches, especially during daylight hours.

"Booth, come down off your hind legs," Danford said. "This ain't no time to go puny and run off, I tell you! We'll cold deck Fargo yet if we just stick together. We got the best pistol and rifle marksmen in the territory in you and Nash, and we still got Red's guns behind us."

"So what? You figure that'll win us coupons in paradise? With the entire country eager to douse our wicks? You and your damn personal grudge against the railroads. This was handled all wrong."

"We've plowed this ground before," Danford shot back. "The thing to worry about now is getting that gold."

Collins loosed a harsh bark of laughter. "You'll see an oyster walk upstairs 'fore you see anymore of that gold."

Skye had been absolutely right, Kristen marveled again as she stirred the mush. The group cohesion of Danford's gang, or what was left of the gang, was crumbling as the pressure mounted. The problem was, that situation could go either way. Since the warning incident last night with the killing of Heck Munro, Danford was tolerating no abuse of her and the children. But if, for example, Collins lost his explosive temper and killed Danford, there would be no one to stop him from venting his rage on her and the kids.

"You're gettin' spooked and giving up on that gold too soon," Danford insisted. "Fargo didn't leave them double eagles last night by happenchance. I think it was a sign that he means to make contact with us soon, offer some kind of deal."

"Hogwash," Collins snapped. "All he's offering us is a noose with thirteen coils in it and a nameless grave on boot hill. For aught we know, there's pony soldiers riding in from Fort Laramie right now to ring these bluffs and trap us."

"That can't happen without Red knowing," Danford insisted. "He's got a headquarters clerk at the fort on his payroll. And later today we're due to get a mirror signal from Red. He's sending one of his men to Middle Fork Creek to send it when the sun is at high noon. We'll have a better notion what to do when we hear from Red."

"In a pig's ass," Collins muttered.

His mean gaze suddenly cut toward Kristen, and he caught her watching him. Suspicion narrowed his eyes.

"You know, Dakota," he remarked, "we only got the ink-slinger's word for it when she claims Fargo didn't contact her last night. He could have slipped her a weapon. I best check her bags one more time."

"Might be a good idea," Danford agreed.

Kristen's blood suddenly turned to ice water, and her heart sat out the next few beats. With baited breath she watched Collins grasp the photo-equipment bag and start pulling the items out.

He gave only a quick glance at the retractable flashpan before tossing it aside. He paused longer over a can labeled FULMINATE OF MAGNESIUM. He pried off the lid and stuck his fingers into the white powder.

"The hell's this?" he demanded, sniffing the powder.

"Who cares, it ain't no weapon, you chucklehead," Dakota said impatiently. "Check the valise."

Kristen prayed silently as Collins snapped open the catches of her valise and rifled through the contents. But once again he missed the secret pocket behind the lining, where the derringer was wrapped in cloth to soften its edges to the touch.

Frustrated, Collins threw the valise down.

"You, mouthpiece," he said to Taffy, who had just woken up. "What do *you* know about what happened last night?"

But Kristen, gambling on a hunch, quickly interceded.

"Leave the children out of this!" she commanded with firm resolve. "They know nothing, I tell you, and neither do I. And I assure you of something else: I intend to make sure the entire world knows how these kids are being treated, and by whom."

"What, you gonna do that from the grave, city princess?"

But, almost miraculously, Collins backed down, walking away in disgust.

This, thought Kristen, is the power and influence of a strong man like Skye Fargo. Without even being present he was actually striking fear into the hard-bitten hearts of these men.

She knew, of course, that she and the children were still in terrible danger. But at least *hope* still lived because of a strong, brave, honorable man willing to shed his blood to protect the innocent. And to think she had once pitied Skye for his lack of education! He was in truth a highly educated master of his domain, the vast and dangerous American frontier. It was she who had shown her ignorance.

"You best get back down that tunnel, Booth," Danford told his hireling. "I'll relieve you after I get the mirror message from Red. Right now I'm going out to spell Nash so he can grab some sleep."

Collins scowled, his twisted mouth like an ugly knife slash. "I still say we should light out now. Take what gold we got and hide out in Mexico. Why let Fargo just pick us off like he done Reece and Heck?"

Danford stubbornly shook his head. "Just remember, Fargo is only dangerous so long as he's free. Just let me get my hands on that slippery bastard one more time, that's all we need. God*damn* him! Next time we snare him, I'll personally kill every one of those little whelps right in front of him if he don't cough up that gold."

His words sent a cold chill down Kristen's spine. Mercifully, Collins disappeared into the tunnel and Danford left the cave by the front entrance to go relieve Nash Johnson.

Kristen crossed to Mattie's pallet and placed a hand on the semiconscious girl's fever-flushed forehead. Still burning up, Kristen fretted, fighting back tears. If Mattie's fever couldn't be broken in the next few hours, the poor child didn't stand a chance.

Six-year-old Ginny lay on the next straw bed, wide awake but totally withdrawn into herself. She still hadn't uttered a word since this horrid ordeal began. As if the poor kid hadn't already suffered enough in her young life. . . .

Kristen knelt to hug her. And to tell her that age-old cliché adults always told worried children, "It's going to be all right, honey, I promise."

Kristen only hoped she herself could really believe that.

It was a standing joke among cavalrymen that their testicles took a beating from long hours in the saddle. For

Fargo, who had spent much of the past twenty-four hours riding hard, the joke was no longer funny.

By the time the sun began to streak the eastern horizon red, he was not only sore, but nodding out in the saddle. Despite the great temptation to stop and sleep, he forged on toward Cheyenne Creek. A child lay dying. Besides, another time factor was critical: He had made a deal with Ike Stockwell and his posse—only thirty-six more hours to rescue those kids Fargo's way.

Eventually, however, still about an hour south of Cheyenne Creek, Fargo nodded out and literally slumped out of the saddle. He landed in an ungainly pile on the ground.

"That tears it," he informed the Ovaro, who had circled back to stand over him. "I'll never make the climb up that bluff without drinking some cowboy coffee first."

The sun was up now and he knew Bolton's men were prowling the area. Fargo built a small fire under a ledge to hold down the smoke, using crumbled bark he kept in a saddle pannier for kindling.

He never had learned to make coffee that didn't taste like river bottom, but he boiled it strong, strong enough to float a horseshoe. Two piping-hot cups, and he was alert again.

He reached the dense woods surrounding Cheyenne Creek without incident. He stripped his saddle and bridle from the Ovaro, quickly drying off the tired stallion with handfuls of bunch grass. Then he tethered his mount in a well hidden patch of graze.

Using whatever hummocks and slight depressions he could find for cover, Fargo worked his way from the woods to the face of the bluff. His left leg was still stiff and sore, but he began the arduous climb up the staircase ledges. Soon he was pouring sweat, but a brisk wind dried it almost as fast as it formed.

A small brown bottle filled with quinine powder was stuffed into his boot. He hoped he was in time to help Mattie. But too late or not, he resolved as he hauled himself laboriously upward, it was high time to fish or cut bait.

Dakota Danford had started this whole mess. Now Fargo meant to end it—and damn quick.

* * *

Kristen was fanning Mattie to cool the child when she heard it, the spooky hooting of an owl.

Elation sang in her blood. Collins and Danford were on guard duty, and Nash Johnson was snoring nearby, making a racket like a boar in rut.

"Taffy, I'll be right back," she said, standing quickly and smoothing her skirt with both hands. "You're in charge."

"Tell that owl I said hello," Taffy remarked, sending her a wink that made her flush. How much, she wondered, has he figured out?

She hurried out to the pond, her face brightening when she saw Skye. But she was shocked by the dark circles under his eyes, the drawn look of his face.

"Am I in time?" he greeted her, handing over the medicine bottle.

"Oh, Skye! Thank God! Wait, I'll be right back. Mattie must get a dose right away."

She returned a minute later and gave him a tight hug, drawing strength and hope from this hardknit man who didn't have the word "surrender" in his vocabulary.

"You're a godsend, Skye Fargo. I think you may have just saved Mattie's life. I'll know in a few hours."

"Maybe we've saved her for now," he qualified. "But we ain't out of the woods yet. How do things stand after my little visit last night? I notice you're still coming and going without too much trouble."

"Oh, they're edgy, all right," she assured him. "And I'm not allowed out of the cave after dark now, none of us are. But luckily they're very busy standing guard during daytime. They still don't know you found a new way up. So most of the time Booth Collins is guarding the rear tunnel, Nash Johnson the front trail."

Fargo swiped at a wispy tress of blond hair that had come loose from the tight knot on her nape, trailing over her cheek. "And Danford?"

"He relieves the other two for short naps. I also heard him tell Collins he's expecting some sort of mirror signal today at noon from Red Bolton."

"So that's how they been staying in touch. It wasn't just that rear tunnel."

Fargo wondered why he hadn't considered this possibility. The U.S. War Department was using mirror stations to good effect down in the arid Southwest, where cloud coverage was minimal. Mirror signals offered limited, but fast, communication that could be relayed for hundreds of miles.

"They buried Heck Munro this morning. Whatever you did to him seems to have greatly unsettled them, especially Johnson. Even Danford. He won't tolerate any abuse of me or the children."

"For now, and that was the point of what I did. But that might not hold. They're too desperate."

She snuggled against him, her breasts soft, pillowy cushions pressing pleasantly into his torso.

"Terribly desperate," she agreed. "And suspicious of me. They fear we're somehow 'in cahoots,' as Collins put it. This morning they even searched my belongings a second time, fearing you had given me a weapon."

This reminded Kristen of her dilemma with the derringer. Worried on that score, she told Fargo about it and asked for his advice.

"I'd just leave it be now. It's easy enough to flash a gun, but sometimes they only make things worse. Besides, they've missed it twice. You turn it over now, they *will* figure we're in cahoots. As it is now, they only suspect that. Why place yourself at greater risk?"

He paused, then added, "And for the love of Pete, if you ever do break out that gun, make sure you intend to use it. Otherwise, don't touch it. But this entire situation has got to be resolved, Kristen. Tonight. For one thing, there's a bound-for-glory citizen's posse about to swoop down on you. Sometime tomorrow, I figure."

She paled at this news. "There's a good chance Collins and Danford will slaughter us if that happens. They know they're going to hang anyway. And they're both vindictive men."

Fargo nodded. "Truth is, they're also brain sick. And logic don't apply to a sick brain. So it's got to be tonight. Late, when they'll least expect it. I've got a string of horses coming later to carry you and the kids. But we'll have to have that front trail clear. With luck I can take care of the sentry. The tricky piece of work for me will be getting into the cave unnoticed. Is it kept lit?"

"They keep one kerosene lantern burning all night, but

turn the wick very low as it gets later. But Danford will probably be there, and he'll be awake. And Collins will be nearby guarding the rear tunnel. He's a deadly shot, Skye, I saw him practice one morning. And Heck Munro mentioned that Collins was once a trick shooter for a circus back east."

"He's a shootist, all right," Fargo agreed. "He wounded me with a pistol at rifle range, and I was rolling and bobbing in fast water."

He had already identified Collins as the greatest threat with a short gun. But Danford, too, worried him. The man was sick, but no coward.

"You'll have to have the kids ready to make a break for it," he told her. "Talk to the older ones and make sure they stay awake. Tell them they'll be responsible for helping the youngest kids. If we move quick, we can get out before Booth Collins even knows what's happening. Besides, he just might decide to save his own skin if he hears trouble in the cave. He ain't loyal to nobody. My big problem is going to be taking care of Dakota Danford before he can hurt you or those kids."

Kristen recalled something. "Skye? I did hear Danford tell Collins that he expects you to approach them and offer some kind of deal for that gold. He hopes to capture you again. He said, he said he'd kill the kids one by one right in front of you if you don't surrender the ransom money. Yet, I know in my bones he'll kill us the moment he does have it, if he can. You were smart to hide it."

"Yeah, we're caught twixt the sap and the bark," Fargo agreed. "But that's good to know, that business with Danford expecting me to offer a deal. I'll ponder that one. You just talk to the kids today, all right? Get them ready in their heads. No matter how it shakes out tonight, you'll all have to move quick when I give the word."

Impulsively, she stretched way up on her tiptoes and kissed him. "I've learned to trust you."

Their eyes met and held. Suddenly, perhaps because it was now broad daylight, she flushed at the memory of their recent passion in this very spot. Especially the bold way she had pleasured him with her mouth.

"I don't normally behave like some bedizened hurdy-gurdy girl," she assured him. "I'm really a good girl, Skye,

Daddy's little angel. But for some reason, when I'm around you, my halo becomes a strap-on model."

Fargo grinned at her joke. "I ain't so sure of that. *I* was sure in heaven for awhile."

He held her out at arm's length. His eyes slowly traveled the length of her, from the luxuriant blond hair to those slim, well-turned ankles. Then back up to dwell on those Grand Tetons swelling out the bodice of her dress.

"You like looking at me, don't you, Mr. Skye Fargo?" she teased him.

"I tend to look at plenty of things, Miss McKenna. But to answer your question, hell yes, I like looking at you. That bother you?"

"Oh, it bothers me, all right, but not the way you mean. It shames me, the pictures I get in my mind when you look at me the way you are now."

In turn, her eyes rushed over him. Then she took a more lingering look at those startling lake-blue eyes, those slim hips and broad shoulders, the strong, bearded jaw. He had an air of . . . readiness, she decided. A relaxed and calm manner, but with a confidence and hair-trigger alertness. Exactly the kind of man she and the children needed at a time like this.

"I shouldn't feel this way about a rough and untutored bachelor of the saddle," she confessed, baiting him with her coquettish smile. "And that's all you'll ever be, isn't it?"

"It's true I've had reins in my hands most my life. And itchy feet, too. Never could reason out how come you town dwellers want to crowd and hobble yourselves the way you do."

"Skye! You're looking at me that way again! I declare, you make me tremble."

Fargo didn't really smile at that, he just twitched his lips a little. "I'm storing you up in my mind."

"Why?"

"For later use," he replied cryptically.

"Meaning . . . ?"

This time he gave her a full, teasing grin. "You wouldn't be turning beet red like that if you didn't already know that answer. 'Course, you being daddy's little angel and all, I s'pose you always sleep with your hands outside the blankets?"

This boldness unsettled her so much that she tried to

give him a playful little slap. But Fargo merely caught her wrist, laughed, and swept her up for another deep kiss.

"And now," he said, releasing her and picking up his Henry, "this conversation has gone as far as it should, girl. It's broad daylight, and we're headed for trouble if I don't skedaddle. I need to get some sleep before I meet Danny, the boy who'll be bringing the horses. You just remember everything we discussed and make sure those children are ready to make tracks when I give the word."

So far the threat from Red Bolton and his crooked vigilantes had remained mostly in the background. But, for Fargo, all that was about to change dramatically.

Most of his climb down the face of the bluff went smoothly. He was still about halfway down when, from the direction of Middle Fork Creek, he detected a series of bright, glittering flashes.

The mirror signal Danford's been watching for, he realized. Whatever news Bolton was signaling, it was in some private code that didn't appear to be Morse. But Fargo knew it could only spell trouble.

That delay to watch the signals proved costly. He still had thirty yards or so to climb when a patrol of six riders suddenly appeared out of a boiling dust cloud from the west. Fargo spotted their big tin stars and immediately realized his luck had finally run out. One of Bolton's roving patrols had finally caught him, exposed and in the open.

At the moment, he was awkwardly preoccupied in clinging to hand- and footholds, unable to shrug the slung rifle off his back or even to grab his Colt. He could only continue climbing down as fast as he could, trying to reach a protective cluster of boulders at the base of the steep bluff. He needed both arms to do it.

The riders bore straight toward him in a rapid beeline, opening fire while still well out on the flats. Clearly Bolton's toadies still had orders to kill him on sight. Bullets splatted against the rocks, some angling off in deadly ricochets that whined close to his ears.

Fargo literally dropped for the last twenty feet or so, managing to land on his feet catlike despite the sharp stab of pain in his wounded left leg. And now his life depended once again on the capabilities of his 16-shot Henry.

Over and over he levered and fired, the Henry's well oiled mechanism performing with flawless reliability. One shell sticking in the breech right now could mean his death. But his wall of lead was having some effect. One man, wounded in the shoulder, peeled away from the charging patrol and headed due south.

Encouraged, Fargo took aim at a rider on a fast blood-bay stallion. He had not had time to adjust his sights for windage, and the bullet hit low, wounding the rider in the shin. But this second hit was enough to break the charge and send the rest of the attackers south behind their fleeing companion.

So Red Bolton's men finally caught up with me, Fargo thought. Yet, they hadn't put up much resistance once he started plinking at them. That was a good sign. Unlike Danford's bunch, Bolton's men didn't seem so eager to follow orders. As the pressure mounted, a firestorm fanned by the newspapers, perhaps Bolton's ragtag army of vigilantes were starting to have second thoughts.

Fargo knew that all this gunfire had to have alerted the sentries up above. But his present position could not be spotted easily from directly overhead, so he decided to lay low for a bit. His face was powder-blackened, his skull still ringing from the constant slapping of the stock each time he had fired. His right shoulder socket was raw from the constant recoil. And the wiping patch he sent down the bore of the Henry actually sizzled from the heat.

When he judged it to be safe, Fargo snuck back across to the nearby woods. The effect of his hot coffee earlier had worn off, and now exhaustion left the Trailsman lightheaded. First he quickly finished cleaning and reloading the Henry. Then he dug out a little sleeping wallow under some chokecherry bushes, covering himself with leaves.

One way or the other, he told himself as he drifted down a long tunnel into blessed sleep, it'll all be over tonight.

12

Under normal circumstances Skye Fargo could fall asleep secure in the knowledge that some reliable inner mechanism would always rouse him at any time he needed to wake up.

There were occasions, however, when prolonged sleep loss and sheer exhaustion made reliance on this natural ability unwise. So before he burrowed into his sleep wallow, he had borrowed an old trick from the Cheyenne Indians. Notoriously late sleepers, they would often drink large amounts of water on nights before battles. Thus, the need to relieve their bladders would wake them in time to seek glory in combat.

Fargo had drunk more than half a canteen full of water before he nodded off. And sure enough, the aching insistence in his bladder woke him up by late afternoon. He was still tired, but more determined than ever to finally end this standoff with Dakota Danford.

He relieved himself, then fed the Ovaro a hat full of parched corn. Fargo hadn't enjoyed a hot meal since this ordeal began. Once again he made do with jerked beef and some hardtack that tasted like it had been growing mold since Adam lost his rib.

He inspected the Ovaro's feet before saddling the stallion. A small stone had become embedded in the left rear hoof, but had not yet caused a crack to develop. Fargo sharpened a twig and carefully pried it out, thankful he had caught it in time. This was no time to be riding shank's mare.

He glanced at the slant of his shadow and judged the time to be about four p.m. Fargo quickly rigged the Ovaro and led him to the southern boundary of the woods. Satisfied that no riders were patrolling close by, he forked leather and booted the pinto up to a lope, bearing toward Middle Fork Creek, the midway point between the town of Bear Creek and Devil's Catacombs.

He found Danny Ford patiently waiting for him. Five horses were tethered behind a windbreak of dwarf willows, contentedly grazing the lush grass.

"Just like you ordered, Mr. Fargo," the eager youth greeted his hero. He wore sturdy trousers of bleached canvas and a butternut-dyed homespun shirt. "Good mounts, but small and gentle. Not a one over fourteen hands."

Fargo nodded, appraising the horseflesh as he dismounted and threw the bridle so the Ovaro could drink.

"They'll do to take along," he assured Danny. "Good work, son. You've been a strong right arm to me, Danny."

The kid flushed with pride, flashing his snaggletoothed grin.

"Seen any riders?" Fargo added.

"Twice. Bolton's men both times. About six in the first group, four in the second. The second bunch crossed here, but didn't spot me nor the horses behind these willows."

"Good man. That means they still aim to ambush me. We'll have to keep our noses to the wind when we head north."

"We?" Danny repeated, unable to believe his ears. "You mean I'm finally gonna get to side you?"

"No need to look so eager, colt. It won't be a trip to Fiddler's Green, I'll warrant that. I wouldn't involve you, except those kids will need your help. You've got to understand from the get-go—this is a dangerous business, not some silly yarn in a penny dreadful. I mean to keep you safe, Danny, if I can. But if this thing tonight comes a cropper, you could get hurt, even killed. You understand that?"

Danny, his face set with determination, nodded. "It don't matter, Mr. Fargo. I can't hardly sleep nights, worrying 'bout them kids. I lost my ma and pa, too. I know what it's like to be all alone in the world."

For a moment, the lad's simple, heartfelt words made Fargo gaze out across the vast, rolling terrain, as if some dark chord of memory had just been plucked.

"I know you do, Danny," he finally replied, tossing an

arm over the gangly youth's bony shoulders. "But you *are not* alone, remember that. Slappy thinks the world of you. And he won't take too kindly to me if I get you shot up. So we got to have some strict rules here, hey?"

The kid nodded.

"All right," Fargo continued, "rule number one: when we get to the woods around Cheyenne Creek, *you wait there* with the horses until I send a signal down from the trail that leads up to Devil's Catacombs. You'll have to watch close and constant—the all-clear signal will be a match lighting. That means you're safe to bring the horses up as far as the head of the trail—*no farther*. You got that?"

Again the kid nodded, concentrating on every word.

"If there's no signal from me," Fargo resumed, "you just stay put. Your job, if and when you come up there, is to help Kristen McKenna get the kids onto horses. They'll be scared, confused. Then you get the hell outta there quick as you can, but be careful going down. These kids are city whippersnappers, and I doubt they know a cantle from a pommel. You'll be the only Westerner among 'em, son, and it may become your job to see they get safely back to Bear Creek."

"Sure I will," Danny vowed. "But won't you be coming with us?"

Fargo sure as hell hoped so. But he had to prepare the kid for the worst.

"Danny," he explained, "there'll likely be some gunplay. And I may have to hang back to cover your escape. But that's none of your picnic, understand? You just stay frosty and don't lose your head, no matter what happens. If it goes bad and I'm killed, you just light a shuck out of there. With the kids if they show up, without them if they don't. No foolish heroics, promise me?"

"My hand to God, Mr. Fargo."

Fargo nodded. "All right, then. We got plenty of time before we have to set out."

Fargo knelt and dug his fingers into the damp red clay beside the creek. He slapped plenty of it on Danny's face.

"Your skin is pale and will reflect the moonlight," he explained. "So we're gonna turn you into an Injun, paleface."

121

"I'll be damned!" Danny exclaimed, still not believing his luck. "I'm gonna side the Trailsman!"

"Normally, I'd swat a youngster for cussing like that," Fargo told him, still busy smearing Danny's face with clay. "But tonight you'll be pulling a man's freight, so I'll let it pass."

"Got a chaw?" Danny added.

Fargo scowled. "Don't push your luck, you little rapscallion. I might still fan your britches."

Kristen McKenna had lived with fear since this awful ordeal began several days ago. But a terrifying new development had brought her to the verge of hopeless panic: the unexpected arrival of Red Bolton, a dangerous man she'd been hearing plenty about lately.

He had arrived without warning earlier in the afternoon, and he and his cousin had been arguing on and off ever since. Right now Bolton was nervously pacing back and forth at the back of the cave. He was a splayfooted man built like his cousin, powerful-chested and heavy, most of it solid muscle.

"I'm telling you, Dakota," he insisted, "I never expected trouble from Fargo when he first drifted into Bear Creek and hired on for the railroad as a guard for Maitland. The man was standoffish, but quiet and polite, and I didn't figure out until too late that the son of a bitch is tough as a two-bit steak. Else I'd've snuffed his flame early on."

Danford, seated on a packing crate with the dead Heck Munro's rifle pointing toward the cave entrance, nodded glum agreement.

"He's savage as a meat ax when he needs to be," Danford admitted. "But we know that now. He won't honeyfuggle us again."

"Balls!" Bolton exploded. In his nervous agitation he kept whacking his boot with a rawhide quirt, the sound grating on Kristen's nerves. "I say we all make tracks now, this very night! Forget about that gold, Dakota. It ain't just Fargo now. That damned Pendergast has been egged on by the newspapers. I heard that arrest warrants is being drawed up. Warrants for me, you, even John Does for some of my men. Face it, cousin, our cake has turned to dough. Now it's time to save our hides."

Kristen found one bit of solace in Bolton's arrival—it sounded as if Skye must still be alive. She had been frightened for him ever since that terrible gun battle she'd heard earlier today, right after Skye left her out at the pond. But he was coming back this very night, totally unaware that Bolton's gun was now added to those aimed against him.

Danford stubbornly shook his head, still resisting his cousin's argument.

"Damn, Red," he said, "I never expected, when I watched for your signal earlier, that you'd be showing yellow and throwing in with us—not after all the work you sunk into getting control of Bear Creek. Don't get me wrong, you're handy with a barking iron, so I 'preciate the extra gun. But with you in charge down in town, we had Fargo trapped in a pincers."

"Showing yellow?" Bolton repeated, anger spiking his tone. "Trapped? Dakota, at least pre*tend* you got more brains than a squirrel! Ain't nobody traps Skye Fargo. That bastard is trickier than a Digger Indian. I'm telling you our hand is played out. Either we make tracks tonight, or as sure as sun in the morning, we're gone beavers."

"I told you," Danford persisted, "I'm sick and tired of always gettin' nothin' but the little end of the horn. Took me five years to build up that sweet little operation with Overland Stage and Freighting. Then the high and mighty in the railroad bought them out and cashiered my ass. *No*, damnit! We'll wait out this night, see if Fargo makes contact. If he don't, then all right, I guess gettin' that gold just ain't in the cards for us, Red. Then we'll follow your plan."

Bolton lowered his voice, but Kristen heard his chilling words. "And them?" he said, nodding toward the captives.

"They're my lookout," Danford replied. "If we don't get our prize, I'll be damned if them railroad dough bellies will get theirs. Not alive, anyhow."

Bolton shook his head in disbelief. "Right there is your problem, Dakota. You put personal grudges before common sense."

"You harken and heed, Red. If I do get that gold, I'll let the damn brats go if there's no way around it. But not Fargo. You let a man like him live, once he's got a dicker with you, and you'll never sleep peaceful again. A man can give the law the slip, eventually, the law forgets. But a man like Fargo will hound you into hell to settle a score. Besides, Booth won't never let him live after the way Fargo laid his face open with that shovel."

"I'm with you on the part about Fargo," Bolton agreed. "I druther have a band of Comanches after me."

"Siddown, Red!" Danford snapped. "Hell, it gives me the fidgets just watching you pace. And quit whackin' your boot with that quirt. Look, just calm down, wouldja? Booth is watching the escape tunnel, Nash is on guard out front. Both those boys could shoot a cootie at five hunnert yards. Plus we've moved the horses down off the bluff. They're waiting outside the tunnel in case we got to hightail it in a hurry."

Those words seemed to mollify Bolton a bit. He did finally sit down on an empty powder keg, planting his solid back next to the rock wall. One hand quirled the ends of his longhorn mustache while the other held his Smith & Wesson six-shooter at the ready.

Kristen felt sick with dread. It wasn't just the arrival of Red Bolton that would complicate Skye's job tonight. The gang had taken other precautions, too. The light within the cave had been cut to a couple of tallow candles. Long, eerie shadows played on the walls.

More ominously, she and the kids had been put directly in the line of fire. They had been forced to stack their straw pallets in the middle of the cave, between the entrance and the rear where the men were holed up. It would be easier for a blind man to thread a needle than to get a bullet safely past her and the kids from outside the cave.

There was at least one ray of sunshine in all this gloom. Thanks to Skye's timely delivery of the quinine, Mattie's deadly fever had broken in the nick of time. She was fully conscious now, and had even taken a little nourishment.

Kristen discreetly gave her another dose now, dissolving the powder in a dipper of water.

"That medicine makes my ears ring," Mattie complained in a whisper to Kristen.

"I know, hon, but it's good for you. That's the girl, drink it all down."

But had Skye saved this sweet little child, Kristen fretted secretly, only so she could die a violent death at the hands of these brutal killers, along with the rest of the kids?

Her gaze shifted to the photography-equipment bag. Earlier she'd had an inspiration about possibly helping Skye at the crisis moment. The equipment was now ready in case she had the chance to do just that.

She had also surreptitiously removed the derringer from her valise. It was now a hard, uncomfortable presence tucked inside her pantaloons. She wanted it handy in case it was needed. And as Skye had suggested, she had quietly spoken to the kids, trying to get them mentally prepared for rescue.

Rescue . . . the notion seemed like an impossible dream now, a fool's quest. Skye was all alone against four cold and desperate killers. Yes, he was an extraordinary man, indeed "a gentleman unafraid." But he was, after all, only a man—not a magician.

Kristen turned her face toward the dark maw of the cave entrance, where the night sky glittered with brilliant starlight. One fact did comfort her—win, lose, or draw, long odds be damned, Skye Fargo was out there somewhere, putting his life on the line for her and the kids.

Fargo and Danny waited in the dense woods near Cheyenne Creek with their string of horses, watching the buttercolored moon slowly crawl toward its zenith. When he judged it was late enough, Fargo left the Ovaro in Danny's care and headed on foot toward the steep trail leading up to the Devil's Catacombs.

Fargo trusted the sure-footed Ovaro. But four feet were more likely to make a sound than two. Sticking to the shadows, using wind noise to cover his advance, he moved quickly up the trail.

He carried his Henry in his left hand, a newly selected club in his right. This would have to be done with absolute silence or he would lose the crucial element of surprise.

He eased around the final turn in the switchbacking trail, and suddenly Nash Johnson was profiled against the night sky. Fargo saw the red glowing eye of Johnson's cigarette, recognized the outline of his Volcanic rifle. Best of all, the sentry had crawled out onto a shelf of rock that jutted about six feet from the lip of the bluff.

Fargo had to slip past him, then around behind him, a tricky piece of work. Luckily, Johnson was evidently bored and tired. He also expected any unwelcome arrivals to be mounted, and he was not being fully vigilant.

Fargo eased past him at a careful crawl, feeling for any loose rocks that might slide and give him away. He had just started to advance forward toward the ledge when a sudden voice from outside the cave made him freeze like a hound on point.

"Nash! Choke that butt, you fool!" Dakota Danford called out. "You tryin' to give Fargo an easy target?"

"Fargo can kiss my lily-white ass," Johnson retorted in a surly tone. However, he did flip the butt away. Fargo watched it disappear into the black void below in a glowing arc.

Damn, Fargo thought, I hope Danny doesn't confuse that with my signal.

"Fargo's more likely to kick your ass than to kiss it," Danford reminded his flunky. "Keep your eyes peeled."

Fargo waited until Danford had ducked back into the cave, then he silently laid his Henry down, gripped the club in both hands, and crept toward the ledge on cat feet.

He swung the club with plenty of muscle behind it, and there was a solid *thuck* when it connected with Johnson's head. The man gave a soft, surprised grunt, then slumped into an unconscious heap.

For the sake of the captives Fargo had been forced to kill Heck Munro in order to send a crystal-clear warning to the gang. But a close glance at the ugly gash over Johnson's ear assured him this man was out of the fight for some time to come, and would probably be useless for days even if he did recover. So Fargo bound his wrists and ankles tight with rawhide thongs, then gagged Johnson good with his own filthy bandanna. For the final touch, he propped Nash up and put the club in his hands so he would still cut the silhouette of an armed man on guard.

Whatever happened tonight, the gang would not be bothering with an injured man who was useless to them. Johnson would answer to the law and meet his fate on a wooden scaffold. Fargo had no desire to play God or cheat the hangman.

He heaved the Volcanic far out into the night, knowing the drop was so long nothing would be heard in the cave when the rifle landed far below.

Fargo waited until the wind had died down. Then he pulled a phosphor from the leather pouch on his belt and held it up, thumb-scratching it to life. He hoped Danny was staying alert below and had seen it, and that the kid would follow orders, bringing the horses no farther than this point.

"Time to get 'er done," he muttered to himself.

Fargo picked up his rifle and headed toward the cave.

Taffy waited until Dakota Danford and his recently arrived cousin were huddled together, arguing quietly but intensely about something they wanted no one else to hear. When they weren't paying close attention, he scooted closer to Nick's pallet. It was sometime after midnight, and the youngest children were asleep.

"I don't know about you, b'hoy," Taffy whispered, speaking in the slang and accent of Lower Manhattan's tough Five Points neighborhood, "but I don't much like that moll buzzer Booth Collins."

Nick had a new bruise on his right cheek where Booth had cuffed him earlier.

"He's a bully and a blowhard," Nick agreed, his dark eyes flashing angry fire. "I hate his pig guts."

Taffy nodded. He had considered approaching Liam with his plan because Liam was a year older than Nick. But Nick was scrappier and had a better throwing arm. And Booth's latest temper tantrum, which had been directed at poor Nick, had finally pushed Taffy to the brink of his endurance.

"There's just so much crap a feller can eat," Taffy went on.

For a moment his eyes cut to a double-bitted ax that Nash Johnson had carelessly left propped against a side wall after he'd split firewood earlier.

"Listen," Taffy added, "he'll be coming in for coffee soon. And he'll start in on us again. When he does, what say me 'n' you fix his flint?"

Nick looked interested. "Yeah, but how?"

Earlier, Kristen had spoken to the three oldest children about a possible escape attempt tonight. But after the arrival of Red Bolton, she had confided her fear to Taffy that Skye Fargo might not be able to challenge so many guns, especially now that she and the kids were directly in the line of fire. But she believed he was out there somewhere, watching and waiting.

So just maybe, Taffy told himself, *we* can get the frolic started for him.

"How?" he repeated. He nodded toward the ax. "Like I said, Collins will be coming in for coffee. Put a few stones in your pockets. When you hear me give the whistle, ship 'em right toward his ugly skull. That'll give me time to grab that Paul Bunyon and start cuttin' down trees, *if* you take my meaning?"

Nick looked tempted. But he glanced toward Bolton and Danford, who still had their weapons handy.

"What about *them* mugs?" Nick asked.

Taffy shrugged. "One of them will take Booth's place in the tunnel. Besides, they plan to croak all of us anyhow. I'm damned if I'll let them shit heels slaughter me like some stupid cow that don't even put up no scrap. I'm goin' down fightin' like a man. And Kristen thinks her friend is outside right now. Betcha anything he'll be able to pitch into the game if we can do in Collins."

Nick thought about it. Then a look of hard resolve shaped his young face.

"That flap-eared egg sucker has been askin' for trouble," he said. "So let's *give* him some."

"Attaway, b'hoy!"

"Hey! You two mouthy mutts!" Danford yelled at them. "Who told you to start flapping your gums? Get away from each other before I clean *both* your clocks! Get to sleep."

Taffy moved back to his pallet. For a moment his gaze met the pretty but troubled blue eyes of Kristen McKenna.

She looked a question at him. But Taffy only gave her a little wink.

Outside the cave entrance, the black velvet night sky seemed to hold its own troubling secret.

13

"I'm telling you, we'll never reach the Mexican border alive," Red Bolton insisted yet again. "You ain't been in town these past few days like I have. Them reporters been popping up around Bear Creek like toadstools after a hard rain. It's almost eight hundred miles to the border from here. How the hell you expect to cover that much landscape when there'll be a manhunt for us in every county we pass through?"

Kristen, pretending to be resting, could still hear the two cousins talking even though they tried to keep their voices down. But no matter how heated their argument became, they rarely took their attention off the front entrance of the cave. One of the candles had guttered out, and eerie, shape-shifting shadows now filled the big cavern.

"Where would *you* run to?" Danford replied. "At least in Mexico the law can't touch us. And I was in the war down there back in 'forty-seven, I know the area around Vera Cruz."

"Mexico eventually, sure. But only after this thing dies down a mite. This is a foolish time to traipse all over hell. For now, our best chance is the Dakota Badlands. I know a spot we could reach in less than three days of hard riding. We could lay low there until some of the heat blows over. Let our hair and beards grow so's we won't look like the drawings on all the reward dodgers that'll be posted everywhere."

"The Badlands?" Danford protested. "Hell, that area's crawling with Sioux, no boys to mess with. And there ain't nothing there—no game, damn little water, no stores for buying tobacco or liquor."

"I brought a packhorse loaded with food and supplies," Bolton replied. "And I know a perfect spot where I use to hole up when I had my own gang. Whistling Rock, a hollow basalt tower. It's surrounded by dry pans and lava lake beds that don't leave no sign for any trackers. And it's wide open thereabouts. No way a man could sneak up on us there. Even soldiers don't go in on account the Sioux won't let 'em. But I know the leader of their band, a renegade named Running Antelope. He'll let small groups of whiteskins enter if they just pay tribute—a few weapons, some sugar and coffee, and suchlike."

Kristen heard Danford smack his fist into the palm of his other hand. His frustration and desperation were increasing as it grew later and Skye Fargo didn't show.

"We ain't goin' *no*where just yet," he insisted. "Fargo's still around, I tell you. Matter fact he musta got close earlier today. Who knows, maybe he was all set to talk turkey, turn over the gold. Your men made enough racket to wake snakes when they attacked him. Why the hell didn't you call 'em off before you lit out? Might be they scared him off, and we'll never lay hands on that gold."

Kristen flinched hard on her pallet when Bolton, himself frustrated, whacked the quirt hard against his boot. The sound was like a pistol shot in this natural echo chamber.

"If brains was horse shit," Red taunted his cousin, "you'd have a clean corral, you know that? *Gold?* God's garters, Dakota! We'll be damn lucky if a lynch mob don't leave us to rot like vines. This ain't no time to search for will-o'-the-wisp. *Or* to be lollygaggin' around here. As things stand now, we're neither up the well nor down."

"You don't like it," Danford snapped, "ain't nobody holding you here. I told you, I'm waitin' out the night. If we don't get the gold, then we'll follow your plan and dust our hocks toward the Badlands."

Kristen heard Danford heave himself to his feet and walk to the hidden cleft that marked the tunnel entrance.

"Booth!" he shouted into the tunnel. "All clear in there?"

She heard Collins shout something back. Her apprehension grew with each passing moment. No matter how she played the scenes out in her mind, she couldn't see this drama ending happily for Skye, her, or the children.

How could Skye possibly mount a successful attack under the present conditions? Yet, if he made no move by sunrise, her captors would be fleeing to the Badlands. Perhaps, just perhaps, Danford would change his mind about killing the children and simply leave them here—she fervently hoped so. But she knew they'd never leave her behind unless they killed her first. They couldn't take that risk knowing she must have overheard at least some of their plans.

As if things weren't dangerous enough, she suspected Taffy and Nick were planning something reckless. Kristen opened her eyes just enough to glance at the nearby photo equipment bag. She knew she was grasping at straws, but even a straw was better than holding onto nothing.

Danford's tense voice suddenly sliced into her thoughts.

"Red! Did you hear something outside the cave just now?"

"Settle down," Bolton scoffed. "Your nerves are frayed, is all. You just checked on Booth and Nash. Ain't no way up here 'cept past them."

"Fargo's got a knack for gettin' around the impossible," Danford reminded him.

Horrified, Kristen watched him grab little six-year-old Ginny, who was sound asleep, and hold her out in front of him as a shield.

Danford moved cautiously to the cave entrance and peered out into the insect-humming darkness. He glanced to his left, toward the head of the trail, and saw Nash Johnson still sitting in profile, mounting guard.

Danford backed into the cave again and roughly dropped the child, who was now awake and wide-eyed with fright, back onto her straw bed.

"Maybe I am a mite jumpy," Danford admitted as he again took his seat on the packing crate. "If Fargo is out there, he best let us know, and mighty damn soon."

The moment he got his first glimpse inside the cave, Fargo had realized all his previous planning was as worthless as wet gunpowder. He was a day late and a dollar short.

To begin with, Red Bolton had joined the unholy mix. Fargo could glimpse him and Danford, but both men were staying low and keeping the captives in the line of fire. Dirt and pine boughs had been piled up and the straw pallets placed on top, making any shots from outside decidedly risky for Kristen and the kids. That risk was already significant thanks to all the rock walls—ricochet, in such close quarters, could be deadly.

Nor was lighting on Fargo's side. He could see only a few daubs of weak candle light reflected off the damp shale walls.

He had crouched behind a tangled deadfall about fifteen feet from the yawning mouth of the cave. What Fargo hadn't counted on was startling a small animal—possibly a rabbit or raccoon—from its hiding place. It suddenly fled from his presence, making enough noise to draw Dakota Danford to the cave entrance.

Fargo tasted the bile of anger at the way Danford was clutching that little girl as if she were a bone shield. He'd kill those kids as casually as he'd wring a chicken's neck, Fargo was sure of that.

When Danford glanced out toward Nash Johnson's position, Fargo settled the butt plate of the Henry into his shoulder socket and took up the trigger slack. If Danford spoke to Johnson, all bets were off. Fargo could still hit a kneecap without endangering the little girl.

But Danford backed inside the cave again, and Fargo released the breath he'd been holding. That danger had passed. However, a large problem still loomed: how in hell was he going to handle this many-headed monster of a dilemma?

Kristen's words from earlier today now surfaced in his memory: *Danford expects you to offer a deal.* But Fargo had played that buried-gold trick once already, and it wouldn't work again unless he really led them to the gold. Besides, all three men hated him with vindictive passion. There was no way they would let him simply ride away even if he did lead them to gold.

The real question was, would they at least let the captives go? A tradeoff—the gold, and his life, for the seven prisoners.

Fargo reluctantly made up his mind. He opened his mouth to call out to Danford. But suddenly Booth Collins emerged through the cleft in the back wall, and Fargo held his silence, watching and listening.

                              *   *   *

"The hell you mean by deserting your post?" Danford
demanded. "I told you both approaches got to be covered
at all times."

"Ease off, why'n'cha?" Collins snapped. "I just come in
to get a cup of coffee. I should've been spelled by now.
How long you planning to sit on your duff jawing with
Red?"

"How long is a piece of string?" Danford shot back.
"Just do as you're told. I'll be there when I get there."

Collins's mean mouth twisted into a scowl as he poured
coffee into a metal cup. "The hell's biting at you? S'matter,
has Fargo got you spooked?"

"Just shut your gob and get back down that tunnel."

It was obvious to Kristen that Skye Fargo had all of these
men spooked, and Collins, always dangerous, was in an
especially foul mood. He noticed that Ginny, still frightened
from Danford's treatment of her, was awake and softly
crying.

"Pipe down, you damn snivellin' little guttersnipe," he
ordered harshly, kicking her pallet.

"You filthy animal, leave her alone!" Kristen cried out.
"She's just a scared little girl!"

Collins turned his hate-filled eyes on Kristen. "Try this
on for size, Little Miss Pink Cheeks."

One quick flick of his wrist, and the contents of his coffee
cup splashed into Kristen's face. Fortunately for her, the
coffee was only warm, not scalding hot.

But this was the final straw for Taffy. He bolted up from
his pallet, loosing a piercing whistle as he lunged for the
ax propped against the wall of the cavern. Before Booth
could react, Nick had jumped up and bounced a stone off
his head.

Booth yowled like a scalded dog. A moment later that
yowl became an ear-piercing shriek when Taffy buried the
ax several inches deep into his left buttock.

All this happened in mere seconds. Bolton and Danford,
taken completely by surprise and still sitting, only now
began to react. Fargo, meantime, had been moving forward
from the moment when Collins first began picking on
Ginny.

Despite the intense pain distorting Collins's face, his eyes

                              133

blazed with primitive rage and blood lust. Even as Taffy drew the ax back for a second blow, Collins filled his fist with iron. But a sudden shout from Fargo, now standing inside the cavern entrance, saved Taffy in the nick of time by redirecting Collins's aim toward the new arrival.

Fargo knew that only a head shot guaranteed a kill with one bullet. And against a lethal marksman like Collins, the first shot *had* to kill. The Henry bucked in his hands, a neat hole appeared in Collins's forehead, and the killer collapsed like a rag doll. His days of tormenting women and children were over.

By now, however, Danford and Bolton had drawn their shooters and were crouched low, using the milling, confused children for cover.

"Drop down flat, kids!" a desperate Fargo roared out, for he could not find a bead in all the confusion. He was a vulnerable target standing by himself a few feet inside the cave.

Bolton, a triumphant grin splitting his granite face, thumbed back the hammer of his six-shooter. But Kristen McKenna, too, had sprung into action, pulling the flashpan out of the equipment bag.

She squeezed the stiff leather bulb in her right hand, and the flashpan filled with magnesium powder exploded in a blinding flash of light and a puff of smoke. She had aimed it directly at Bolton and Danford, who could now see nothing.

She had just saved Fargo's life, and he knew it. That was one little spoiled city gal with grit in her. Unfortunately, that bright flash had also temporarily blinded him, too.

"Run outside, children!" Kristen shouted desperately.

However, the kids, too, were disoriented by the flash. She hung back to help the still weak Mattie to her feet. Thus, Danford was able to grab hold of Kristen just before he and Bolton, still rapidly blinking from the bright flash, escaped into the tunnel.

"Listen, you high-toned slut," Danford hissed as he pressed the muzzle of his Smith & Wesson into her ear. "If Fargo follows us in here, I'll decorate the walls with your brains! *Tell* him!"

"Skye!" she cried out through the narrow opening. "Save

the children! If you rush the cave Danford will kill me! *Please*, Skye, get the children to safety!"

For a few moments Fargo stood among the scared, confused kids, suffering from a rare moment of indecision. Then the pitiful crying of the littlest children made his duty clear: As much as he hated leaving Kristen with those two jackals, the little ones came first. Kristen understood that, and so did he.

"Let's go, youngsters!" he called, herding them outside. "Hold hands and follow me."

Dependable Danny had done his job to the letter and was waiting at the head of the trail with the string of horses. He, Skye, and Taffy helped the rest of the kids get mounted. Danny put Ginny in the saddle with him while Skye took care of the recovering Mattie, holding her securely in the saddle after wrapping a blanket around her.

For a tempting moment Fargo had considered letting Danny lead the escapees back to Bear Creek while he headed after Kristen. Then he remembered that Bolton's men might still be out there somewhere, following old orders, and the kids would be unprotected. He had no choice but to escort them back to town and stay with them until they were in safe hands.

As they headed down the winding trail, Fargo felt grateful and relieved that the kids were finally free and in reasonably good condition. But he also felt angry, frustrated, and worried about Kristen. By the time he would be able to cut trail on Bolton and Danford, they would have fled to hell and gone.

"You done it, Mr. Fargo!" Danny called out gleefully behind him. "You *done* it!"

"Not quite all of it, Danny," Fargo replied, realizing again that Kristen McKenna had saved his bacon back in that cavern. "There's still one pretty and gutsy lady missing, and I like to finish what I start."

The ride back to Bear Creek was long and tiring, but mercifully uneventful. The deceptive glow of false dawn was visible in the east by the time the exhausted caravan filed down the dark, deserted main street. Mattie was sound asleep against Fargo's chest, and the rest of the kids were nodding out.

135

There was no sign of Red Bolton's men. Maybe by now, Fargo told himself, they realized their "fearless leader" was running like a river after the snow melted. There would be no more trouble from them.

There was only one place to take all these sleepy kids at this late hour—the livery stable. Slappy Hupenbecker grumbled, at first, when Danny shook him awake. But the moment he laid eyes on all those sleepy kids, an ear-to-ear smile split his beard-grizzled face.

"Well, I'll be earmarked and hog-tied! By Godfrey, you and Danny *done* it, Skye!" he exclaimed as he hopped excitedly around, gathering horse blankets to spread in the hayloft so the exhausted kids could sleep. "No forty-rod this time, young feller. Now I break out the high-grade."

Slappy plucked the lid off a nail keg and produced a bottle of Old Taylor. "Mighty smooth sippin' whiskey," he added with a wink.

Later, as a weary Fargo stretched out in the hay beside the already sleeping kids, his gaze rested for a moment on Taffy and Nick. They were the real heroes in the events of this night. It was their courageous actions that finally broke the impasse within the cave—that, and Kristen's literally "brilliant" move with the flashpan, had saved the day.

Fargo still intended to stay wide of cities. But never again would he doubt the toughness or resolve of city kids, nor the ingenuity of city women. They came out onto a wild, unknown frontier with their antlers still green. And yet, when it came down to do or die, by God they *did* it. A man could ask for no more of anyone.

These kids had done their job, he reminded himself as sleep claimed him. But now it was time for him to finish his. A woman who had bravely stuck by the children, and even saved his life, now needed his help.

And by all things holy, she was going to get it. Fargo only hoped he wouldn't be too late.

14

Skye Fargo was still groggy with sleep fumes when the newspaper reporters descended on him like a plague of locusts.

He and the kids had slept for six solid hours, rising around noon and trooping over to the Crossroads Café, Bear Creek's only eating establishment. After a delicious hot meal of beefsteak, fried potatoes, greens, and apple pie, Fargo turned the kids over to an ecstatic Peyton Norwood, the local representative for the Northwestern Short Line. The smiling Norwood was suddenly busy as a moth in a mitten, arranging temporary homes for the children and making flowery speeches to the growing throng of reporters and townies.

Fargo also described, in strict confidence, the area where Norwood's people would find the railroad company's hidden gold, minus $5,000. And even that amount, he added, just might be returned soon. After conferring with Norwood, Fargo had quietly given everyone the slip.

He snuck over to the Drover's Cottage to purchase a hot bath, then headed back to the livery to prepare his Ovaro for the trail. Kristen McKenna's captors already had a good head start on him. He knew time was critical now. For Kristen's sake he had to cut sign on Danford and Bolton as quickly as possible.

However, it didn't take the news hawks long to search him out. Fargo was trimming one of the Ovaro's hooves with a hasp when a group of them burst into the livery, spouting questions nineteen to the dozen.

"Mr. Fargo, how many men did you kill?"

"Mr. Fargo, is it true you charged the Danford gang with your reins in your teeth and both guns blazing?"

"Mr. Fargo, do you fan your hammer like the heroes in the half dimers?"

Fargo exchanged ironic glances with Slappy and Danny.

"Gents, I got no time for jawboning," Fargo replied.

A reporter with a thin, sharp-nosed face stepped aggressively closer. Obviously he fashioned himself a dandy. He wore a cravat with a diamond-headed pin, and there were satin facings on the lapels of his jacket.

"Was Kristen McKenna outraged?" he demanded.

Fargo, unfamiliar with the language of purple prose, expelled a patient sigh. "Of course she's outraged. Wouldn't you be, in her place?"

"No, no, my good man, obviously you don't understand. Was she . . . violated?"

Fargo frowned, no longer patient. "Look, all I know is, she's a good woman with a lot of courage, and she's in a heap of trouble. You *ought* to be worried about her safety, not who's been under her petticoats. Now you either walk right back out them doors, or I'll send you out through the wall."

The reporter drew himself up in a huff. "I, sir, write for the *Kansas City Sentinel*."

"The devil you say!" Slappy exclaimed sarcastically. "Danny, fetch some water so's this holy man can baptize us."

"Why you, Fargo?" the reporter demanded. "I don't see a badge on you. Who appointed you head lawman around here?"

Slappy bristled like a feist. "There ain't nobody else around here with the guts or the caliber to get it done. That's why he's doing it. When's the last time any of *you* chattering magpies looked down the barrel of a gun?"

A thundering silence followed Slappy's outburst.

"Quaint," one of the reporters finally remarked. "He must be the town's 'crusty old codger.'"

"He smells like its crusty old distillery," another japed.

However, when Slappy brandished a pitchfork, the newspaper writers filed out in a hurry.

"Buncha weak sisters," Slappy muttered. "That feller from Kansas City smelled like a French cathouse."

"Mr. Fargo," Danny asked, "where you think them men took Miz McKenna?"

Fargo was busy lashing a gunny sack filled with grain to his cantle. He wouldn't have time to let the Ovaro graze much, if at all. Besides, depending on where he ended up, there might not be much browse except sagebrush.

"Won't know till I cut sign on 'em, Danny boy," he replied. "Maybe south. But I'd wager the passes and water holes will be guarded in that direction."

"They dursn't run to any area that's settled up," Slappy tossed in. "Might be they'll head toward the Yellowstone drainage. Men on the prod tend to hole up there."

"Distinct possibility," Fargo agreed.

"Anyhow," Slappy added, "you've scairt off Red Bolton for good, and I say good-bye and amen, brother! Ever since Bolton got here, innocent people been dyin' of colic, lead colic. You just watch your topknot, Skye. You costed Danford and Bolton plenty, and neither one of them wrathy bastards is likely to forget it soon. Not by a jugful!"

"These horses are about blown in," Red Bolton announced. "And so'm I. We got to rest up awhile."

They had been riding hard since well before sunrise, and by now it was early afternoon. Kristen, unused to horsebacking, felt her muscles cramping from long hours in Nash Johnson's saddle.

"Town living has turned you flabby, Red," Dakota Danford snapped. "You want egg in your beer, too?"

"Mite scratchy today, are'n'cha? You want these mounts to drop dead under us, leave us afoot?"

Danford reined in. "Ahh, it ain't you, Red. I just can't push that gold outta my thoughts."

"Why lick old wounds?" Red said as he swung down and threw the bridle so his claybank could drink from a little seep spring south of the Platte River.

"Old wounds?" In his wrath every vein in Danford's neck stood out like fat night crawlers. "You talk like it was twenty years ago all this happened. Damnit, don't you unner'stan' we was *that* close"—he snapped his fingers—"to a lifetime of ease and plenty? Until Fargo had to meddle in it. All you had to do was plug him when you had the chance."

Bolton, gnawing on a cold biscuit, shook his head as if Danford were a child throwing a temper tantrum.

"To hear you take on about it," he said, "it's the end of the world. Hell, fortunes are like shadows, cousin, hard to grasp and they don't last long. We'll get our chance again. And don't forget, we got that five thousand in gold."

Kristen, too, had dismounted to stretch her muscles. She could feel both men's eyes on her, monitoring her every move. She knew what was on their minds, besides raping and killing her, and Danford spoke up about it now.

"That was a pretty slick plan you and Fargo cooked up, city princess. Poof! One big, blinding flash! And all that time, you had the makin's for that little bomb right there under our noses. Hell, my hat's off to you, gal."

He paused, his eyes raking her. "No wonder we couldn't get you to scent for us. You was meeting Fargo every night, hanh? Lifting up them skirts and lettin' him climb all over you."

Her face flamed with anger and humiliation, but now that the children were no longer her responsibility, she was no longer mistress of her fear. She couldn't have retorted even if she'd wanted to, her mouth felt stuffed with cotton.

At least she had the consolation of knowing Skye had gotten those children to safety at long last. She owed them that because, in part, her writings had placed them in this danger.

As for her own chances, she had finally given up all hope of surviving. True, she still had that two-shot derringer tucked into her pantaloons, and if she got the chance to use it, she would at least try although she had never fired a weapon in her life. But after what Taffy and Nick had pulled last night in the cavern, and then her trick with the exploding flashpan, these two weren't taking their eyes off her. And she'd already heard them agree to tie her wrists and ankles anytime they had to sleep.

Bolton was being especially disgusting. He could make a woman feel like a whore just by the way he leered at her, as he was doing right now.

"Hell, Dakota," he remarked. "Let's strip her buck right now. Looks to me like she's got 'er a top-shelf set of knockers. But you can't tell if the wood is good just by lookin' at the paint. Ask Fargo, right, sweet patooties?"

He reached toward the stays on her bodice, and Kristen shrank back, her heart constricting with fear. If they found that gun, they'd do far worse than rape her.

"Don't worry," Danford told his cousin. "We're gonna make this little filly see God, all right, and we won't even charge her a stud fee. But first let's get to that Badlands hideout of yours. This ain't no time for frippit. Fargo *will* be coming after us, coz, a well-bred dog hunts by nature."

"Let him hunt," Red scoffed. "The reason I picked Whistling Rock is that nobody can draw near it without being spotted. There ain't enough ground cover for a weevil to hide behind, let alone a man. Even darkness won't help him—there ain't no mountains in the background to shadow a man's approach. And once we spot him—"

Bolton nodded toward the Sharps rifle protruding from his saddle scabbard. The big fifty-caliber slugs packed a whopping seven hundred grains of powder, making the weapon virtually a hand-held artillery piece.

"That Big Fifty puts a hole in a man big enough to drive a freight wagon through," Bolton boasted. "Guts won't do Fargo no good once they're blowed out of him."

After the horses had drunk and rested, and the men had a smoke, the trio mounted up again. Bolton nudged his claybank up close to Kristen, a lewd smile distorting his hard features.

"Can't wait to prick the vent," he whispered in her ear, so close she felt the tickle of his mustache and smelled the rancid stench of his unwashed body.

Her skin grained with fear and revulsion, and Bolton tossed back his head, roaring with taunting laughter.

At first, Danford and Bolton had made no effort to cover their escape. Fargo easily picked up the trail on the far side of the bluffs near Cheyenne Creek.

He made out four sets of tracks. He assumed they had put Kristen on Nash Johnson's horse. The fourth horse, he could tell from the increased depth of the tracks, was a well-laden packhorse. Wherever they were headed, they would be well supplied.

The first leg of the journey was fairly easy riding through rolling scrubland. Eventually, however, his quarry began to take every opportunity to obscure their trail and slow him down. They deliberately rode across ground trampled by buffalo herds, cattle, other shod horses. At times Fargo was forced to ride for long periods hunched low in the saddle, his experienced eyes scouring the trampled ground.

Mostly this was wild, wide-open terrain, and he spotted few signs of human civilization. During the first day in the saddle he passed a few half-section nester farms, worked by struggling hoe-men as slat-ribbed as their livestock. He also spotted a convoy of bullwhackers in the distance and one Concord coach rocking on its thoroughbraces.

At one point Bolton and Danford tried to bamboozle him by riding across a huge buffalo wallow crisscrossed with the tracks of many animals and riders. They had divided for a time before they emerged from it in different locations, trying to confuse him. Fargo was forced to dismount and go through the painstaking process of starting at the edge of the tracks and sorting out the single riders. In this way he was able to pick up the exact spot where they joined up again.

The trail bore northeast, and at first he couldn't rule out the forested Black Hills of western Dakota and northeast Wyoming as their destination. However, that struck him as unlikely. Long before white men named these mountains the Black Hills, they had been known to the Sioux as the *Paha Sapa*, the sacred center of the Lakota universe. Bolton and Danford were criminals, all right, but they weren't *that* stupid. A white man would be wiser to ride into hell with his pockets stuffed with firecrackers.

So he guessed, early on, that they were headed for the formidable Dakota Badlands, an eerie, desolate expanse of rock formations and animal fossils. Eventually their trail confirmed it. After they had crossed the North Platte, they followed the Niobrara River due east, skirting the Black Hills on their southern border. Just beyond the farming settlement of Chadron in the Nebraska Territory, they took a jog to the north.

They followed the White River for about half of the remaining distance. Then the White turned eastward, and Skye continued tracking north into the distinctive terrain of the Badlands. During this long journey he never once made a camp, eating in the saddle and stopping only to spell the Ovaro and grab snatches of sleep.

Nor did weather or darkness deter him. It was still so chilly in the early morning that the Ovaro's urine steamed. At one point tendrils of cold rain lashed at Fargo's face, and jagged white tines of lightning forked down to the ground, spooking the pinto. Still, a resolute and determined Fargo pushed on. After dark he oriented, in all this open vastness, by constellations, the polestar, and the dawnstar in the east.

The gently rolling terrain had become mostly flat now. The first massive rock formations had begun cropping up, offering hidden marksmen good cover for a clear shot at anyone caught in the open. Fargo always stayed in motion, stopping only behind cover when he could find it. The wind howled in gusts, and some of the massive rock sculptures whistled and shrieked as the wind got trapped in a thousand fissures and crevasses. Now and then Fargo laid a hand on the Ovaro's neck to calm him.

So far the trail was still clear. But he knew the Badlands, and knew also that as he penetrated deeper into the heart of this desolate expanse, dry pans and lava lake beds would obscure the sign.

Soon, however, Fargo realized he had another problem. Someone was also tracking *him*.

It was a lone rider, staying far enough behind that Fargo rarely glimpsed him. Whoever it was stopped when he stopped, as if content to watch for now. Might be a Sioux warrior, he speculated, sent to keep an eye on him.

Trouble ahead, trouble behind.

"Pile on the agony," he remarked to the Ovaro. "Well, old campaigner, life never gets too boring for us, does it?"

Man and beast pressed forward, as unstoppable as destiny.

15

"That's Whistling Rock straight ahead," Red Bolton announced.

He pointed toward a tall tower of basalt rock that pointed straight up into the sky like an accusing finger.

"I figger we'll reach it in about three or four hours now," he added. "There's a hollow in the base, gives good shelter from the weather. Also hides fires, and there's room to picket the horses."

His hard-bitten eyes shifted to Kristen McKenna. "Once we get there, Dakota, me 'n' you will have us plenty of time for tomcattin' with this queen."

Throughout this entire ordeal, Kristen had never felt such depths of fear and despair as she felt now. The three riders had made a brief camp sometime during the second night, and the dull, leaden light of dawn had revealed a sight she still couldn't quite believe.

She had read a little about the Badlands, but sketches in books paled beside seeing the actual terrain. The sheer lifelessness and silence of the place was eerie and unreal—like a landscape from a bad dream. Roughhewn lava rocks formed grotesque shapes against an overcast morning sky the color of dirty bath water. At least the sun was starting to peek out as the sky began to clear.

"We'll turn to tomcattin' when the time comes," Danford replied, one of his strong Mexican cigars stuck in the corner of his mouth. He had been closely observing their back trail for the past five minutes. "I could be wrong, but I think we got a drag rider out there."

"How far back?" Bolton demanded.

"A far piece yet. I don't see him now. If somebody is following us, you know it's Fargo."

"Just *one* rider?"

Danford nodded.

"Then it don't matter," Bolton pointed out confidently. "He'll never close the gap once we hole up at Whistling Rock. He's got to cross miles of flat, open ground, and we got the Sharps. Sure, he's got that Henry repeater, but it don't matter unless he can get close enough to score hits. Which I ain't gonna let him do. And with him dead, won't nobody else know where to look for us."

This was their last camp before reaching Whistling Rock, and the men were taking no chances. The horses were neither hobbled nor tethered, just standing with their saddles still on and bridles trailing so they could eat from nose bags filled with oats.

"Eat your grub," Danford snapped at Kristen. They had forced her to cook panbread and bacon, but she shook her head, unable to eat any of it. She felt exhausted and filthy, and her eyes were red and swollen from stinging, wind-blown grit. She had no coat, and she was almost warm enough until the wind gusted, cold slicing into her like a knife. And making those awful rocks shriek like damned souls in the process! Oh, dear Lord, she prayed, please don't let that awful howling be the last sound I hear.

"Well now," Bolton taunted, "Little Miss Pink Cheeks seems to be off her feed a mite. We can't have none of that, sweet corset. You'll be needing your strength for later."

He pushed the tin plate under her nose, and Kristen angrily swatted it away. Even her fear couldn't stop her now. She was sick of all this, and just wanted it over one way or the other. "Go to hell!"

Bolton's lips eased away from his teeth in a wolf grin. "Pretty kitty, but a rough tongue. Don't get your bowels in an uproar, sweetheart."

He yanked her to her feet and tried to force his mouth onto hers. Kristen's right knee flew up, catching Bolton solidly in the crotch. He suddenly released her, doubling up and taking in a hissing breath.

"Don't touch me, you murdering piece of dirt!" she spat out.

Despite his own fear and exhaustion, Danford couldn't help howling with mirth when he saw his cousin holding himself and turning green. "Damn, Red, there goes your branch of the family tree. I do belive the ink-slinger just gelded you."

When the pain subsided, he looked at her with angry eyes like molten metal.

"Yessiree," he said in a flat, dangerous tone. "All of a sudden that tongue of hers has been salted in a pickling jar, all right. And I'm thinkin' it's on account she thinks her big, tough hero is riding to her rescue."

Bolton turned to the packhorse and pulled a skinning knife with a curved blade from one of the packs. Kristen felt her pulse leap into her throat.

"Maybe if I peel off a little of that lily-white hide of yours," he said, advancing toward her, "you'll learn to keep a civil tongue in your head."

Danford, during all this, had been studying the terrain to the south. Suddenly he spoke up.

"Red, damnit, never mind the woman for now! Hell, you're as randy as Booth was. I think I see that rider again. Break out the Sharps. Won't be long, he'll be in range."

Whoever was approaching was still a speck against the horizon. Bolton slid the rifle from his saddle scabbard, then turned the horse around a half-turn to use it as a shooting platform. He laid the long barrel of the single-shot breechloader across his saddle and thumbed back the hammer.

He glanced over at Kristen, who had suddenly paled.

"Won't be long," he assured her, "and the coyotes will be gnawing your lover boy's bones."

Skye Fargo never used field glasses in the direction of the sun, knowing that reflection off the lenses carried for miles in open country. But he knew he had been steadily gaining on his quarry and that they couldn't be far ahead of him now. They had made two camps behind natural windbreaks, so far, and the last one he checked had ashes still slightly warm to the touch.

However, the newly risen sun limited his naked vision, and he had deliberately slowed his pace. Clearly Bolton and Danford had a destination in mind or they wouldn't have fled to the Badlands. He didn't want to catch them in the open too soon for fear of what they might do to Kristen if attacked. But it was a delicate balancing act since he didn't want them to reach their destination too soon, leaving them plenty of time to turn their sick attention to her. She was safest when they were preoccupied.

A saddle-weary Fargo, who had been letting the Ovaro walk at his own pace, reined in for a moment to ease the ache in the small of his back. He leaned forward and rested his forearms on the saddle horn, stretching his back. This momentary lowering of his profile saved his life by inches.

He heard the hornet buzz of the passing bullet even before the distant crack of a rifle reached him. Instantly he reined around and retreated, riding in a zigzag pattern to throw off the marksman's next bead.

He jutted a few hundred yards to the west, holing up in a clutch of black rocks. By sheer luck he had happened onto one of the natural hot springs dotting the Badlands. Knowing he needed to delay for a bit anyway, he stripped and eased into the warm, bubbling water, grateful for the opportunity to reinvigorate his tired, aching body. For a time he allowed himself to enjoy feeling as lazy as a lizard on a hot rock.

But Fargo had another motive for his delay. He wanted to give the tracker behind him a chance to approach him peacefully, which the man was obviously hoping to do. By now Fargo had gotten a good look at him through the spyglasses, and he was no longer worried, only curious.

It was a Sioux warrior following him, but whatever his intentions, they were not bloody. No Sioux brave ever attacked an enemy without painting his face and body for battle. This was so crucial to a Sioux, that even the bravest warrior would flee from a fight, without loss of honor, if he hadn't had a chance to paint.

Besides being unpainted, this brave was fully dressed in knee-length moccasins with doeskin leggins and shirt. A Sioux almost always stripped to his clout when he was on the scrap, even in winter. But what really convinced Fargo not to fear an ambush was the brave's distinctive red sash. He was an elite "sash warrior," a member of the Sioux Kit Foxes, among the most honored of the Plains Indians's warrior societies.

Their bravery and honor were as legendary as the bravado of their famous battle cry: "I am already dead!" To show his resolve in battle, a Kit Fox pinned his sash to the ground as a sign that he intended to win or die on that very spot. In Fargo's experience, only the Cheyenne Dog Soldiers, or the Kaitsenko warriors of the Kiowa, could match them in fighting ferocity.

So he knew the brave had some important reason for wanting to make contact with him. And he showed no sign of hostility when, as he expected, the sash warrior eventually peeked cautiously round the rocks at the whiteskin soaking in the hot spring.

Following the Indian custom, Fargo kept his face completely impassive, showing no surprise, fear, or other emotions. He held up one palm in peace. He made no move toward his weapons, which lay on top of his nearby pile of clothing.

The Sioux nodded once and held up a palm. Then he advanced a little closer, leading a small but sturdy pony by a hair headstall. The Ovaro made a nervous nickering sound, for he had whiffed the shiny bear grease in the brave's long hair. The warrior also wore a necklace of bear claws.

Fargo was not fluent in the Lakota tongue. But he knew a smattering of words, as well as some Cheyenne—a language most Sioux understood since the Cheyennes were their cousins and longtime battle allies. If all else failed, Fargo could also resort to sign language to fill in, the lingua franca of the Great Plains.

When the Sioux spoke, he mixed some English with his words and signs.

"I am called Many Coups," the Kit Fox greeted the naked white man. "I do not live among the local Lakota band, who follow the chief Running Antelope. I am on my way to the *Paha Sapa* to purify myself in steam and seek a vision from the High Holy Ones."

Fargo nodded, catching the gist of it. Before he could identify himself, the warrior did it for him.

"I know of you. All red men do. The Dineh, the Navajos far to the south, call you Son of Light. The bearded one who once saved their little ones from slavery. Unlike many *wasichus*, whiteskins, you have no quarrel with the red man. In the way you live, you are much like us."

This was all preliminary politeness. Now the brave sat cross-legged upon the ground. This was a sign that inconsequential remarks were over. Now it was time for serious parley.

Many Coups said, "You know that, despite the talking paper our two people signed, white-eye law does not matter here?"

Fargo nodded. The "talking paper" Many Coups meant was the 1851 Laramie Treaty. According to this treaty, red men and white men were to punish their own malefactors. But like most treaties, it was written on water. Both whites and Indians had broken it many times.

"But the blue-bloused soldiers will not punish those you are after," Many Coups added.

Unsure if he had spoken clearly on this point, he made the sign for white men, pulling a finger across his forehead to indicate a hat brim. Then he held up two fingers and pointed in the direction Danford and Bolton were fleeing.

"You know of their evil?" Fargo asked.

The brave nodded, and Fargo was not at all surprised. Long ago he had discovered the so-called "moccasin telegraph," the Indian system of smoke signals, mirror flashes, and runners that could be remarkably efficient at keeping each other informed of the white man's doings.

"We Lakota," Many Coups continued, "we will kill and torture any enemy without regret. That is the warrior way. But children, even *wasichu* children, are not enemies. They are innocents. Those we capture we take into our tribe and treat as our own blood. These men you are seeking, they are without honor. They do not respect even whiteskin children. Such men are evil medicine, and now they have come too close to our sacred *Paha Sapa*. If they are allowed to live, the Great Mystery above, he who makes the days, will punish us. So this place hears what I swear now: I *will not* let my people suffer for these white dogs."

Fargo gave a solemn nod. "As you say, Lakota. I mean to kill them."

Many Coups nodded. "No better man to do it. However, in this vast, open place your task is hard, and you are alone.

149

I cannot help you directly. I am not purified to kill, nor can I ride into our sacred hills with blood on my hands. Yet, I can give you these."

Many Coups was holding a rolled-up coyote fur. He set it down beside him and opened it up. "We Lakota know how to drive our enemies out of breastworks and other shelters."

There were four arrows made of fire-hardened pine, tipped with flaked flint, and fletched with black crow feathers. But these arrows were far from ordinary.

Fargo nodded, recognizing them: They were "exploding arrows," invented first by the Cheyenne. A percussion cap had been fitted to each arrow point. These were then wrapped in a small cotton sack filled with gunpowder. Upon striking, the flint tip would split the percussion cap, in turn igniting the gunpowder. They did not always work, but Fargo had seen them used to great effect in setting wagons and structures ablaze. The resulting explosion could be quite unnerving—and do serious damage if they struck a human body.

The Kit Fox shrugged the strong, osage-wood bow off his shoulder. It was strung with powerful buffalo sinew.

"You know how to use this?" he asked.

Fargo nodded. A bow of this quality had impressive range and force. He had seen osage bows drive arrows completely through a buffalo, dropping them out on the other side.

"I will fashion another for myself when I reach the *Paha Sapa*," Many Coups said. "Now you can overcome the great problem of distance. Good hunting, Son of Light. May the Holy Ones ride with you into battle."

"Wait," Fargo said as the brave turned to leave. "I cannot take this fine gift without giving one in return."

Many Coups shook his head. "When you kill these evil men, you fulfill the ancient laws of the Manitus. There is no greater gift you can give the Lakota people."

16

The spring water was warm and hard with minerals, but drinkable. Since access to it was limited to a narrow opening in the rocks, Fargo patiently fetched several hats full for the Ovaro.

While his horse drank, Fargo studied the sun. Earlier, it had been to the distinct advantage of his enemies. Now it was a little higher in the sky, but still a problem for Fargo if he continued to track dead ahead into it. So instead, he decided to employ cavalry tactics and "quarter the wind," shifting to an oblique right-angle assault. While it was generally best to attack out of the sun, as Indians always tried to do, he could at least put it out of his eyes.

The key now, he realized, would be speed and aggressiveness. No more cat-and-mouse games, he had to take the fight directly to Danford and Bolton. If they reached a good defensive position, in all this vast openness, that Sharps would spell his death. Worse, Kristen McKenna would suffer unspeakable indignities before they killed her.

Fargo scratched the Ovaro's withers.

"It's been a hard ride, old friend," he told the pinto. "And as always you've been a stout trooper. But I know you've got plenty more bottom left in you. We need it now, boy."

The Ovaro pricked his ears forward, as if listening intently. Over the years an unspoken bond had developed between man and animal. The stallion always seemed to sense the urgency of his master's voice.

Fargo reset his saddle, checked cinches and latigos, swung up into leather. With the bow hooked over his left shoulder, the arrow pouch tucked into his buckskin shirt, he gave the Ovaro a little squeeze with his knees. And the stallion was off like an antelope.

Fargo opened his horse out to a long lope, bearing north-northeast. When the angle of the sun no longer blinded him, he scrutinized the terrain before him with minute attention. Finally, his hawk eyes picked up a tiny speck of motion, off to the east and far out ahead.

Soon Fargo, too, had spotted that tall basalt tower. And since it was the only sizable object for miles around, other than small clusters of black lava rocks, he knew it had to be Danford and Bolton's final destination.

I can't let them get there, he resolved. He had to strike before they reached cover, and hope to God Kristen still had that gun and the will to use it at the right moment.

He dug his heels into the Ovaro's flanks. Although already blowing lather, the plucky steed stretched itself out to a rapid gallop, its will one with Fargo's.

"Won't even be a half hour now," Bolton told Danford, "and we'll be safe and snug. I'm telling you I *hit* Fargo back there a ways. You don't see him dogging our trail anymore, do you?"

"No," Bolton admitted. "But I did see him retreat in a puffin' hurry. I don't think you tagged him, Red. But might be you scared him off. That's damn near as good."

"Thank old Patsy Plumb here," Bolton bragged, patting the wooden stock of the Big Fifty. "Even a hellhound like Fargo ain't crazy enough to ride into the teeth of a Sharps. That Henry he's totin' will fire all week long without reloading. But that tubeloader is awkward and clumsy to extract and load, and besides, it's a pea shooter up agin' a smoke pole like this."

Bolton turned his dead-as-buttons eyes toward Kristen. "I *owe* Fargo one. He jumped me in my own office when my back was turned, coldcocked me. I mean to settle that score by dangling his scalp off my belt."

He laughed when their prisoner paled slightly. "Aww, poor city princess! All worried about her hero when she's got big troubles of her own. You know, Dakota, I commence to wonder that as long as we're eventually heading into Mexico anyhow, maybe we should keep this little filly alive and enjoy her on the trip down? You know how wild them Mexers are for blondes with big knockers. Hell, we could sell her on the market for upwards of a thousand dollars."

Such talk hardly fazed her now. But Kristen felt an ice-cold ball of fear in her stomach as they neared their destination. She felt like a damned soul on the threshold of hell. Now she realized what the ultimate purpose of her hidden derringer must be: to take her own life quickly rather than let these beasts ravage and kill her.

As much as she admired Skye, she couldn't help a keen sense of disappointment and abandonment now. He had come so far, hung in there through all these hard days of fighting. How could he just give up—

"God in whirlwinds!" Danford exclaimed.

Kristen nearly leaped from her saddle in fright as an arrow suddenly thwacked into the heaped load on the pack-horse, exploding in a burst of flame! Despite its heavy load, the animal suddenly reared up on its hind legs, whickering in fright and showing the whites of its eyes.

Cursing, Bolton used the leadline to gain control of the panicked gelding. "What the—?"

"There!" Danford shouted, pointing off to their left. "That crazy Fargo is attacking us! And he's using a bow and arrows!"

"Arrows, my sweet aunt!" Bolton replied, leaping down from the saddle and sliding the Big Fifty from his saddle sheath. "I'll knock that bastard clear into next week. Put them flames out, Dakota! I got two ammo belts in there somewhere."

Bolton couldn't get his nervous horse to stand still long enough to steady the long gun on its back. So he took up a prone position, digging in his left elbow. But Fargo, racing ever closer, didn't make an easy target as his pinto ran a zigzagging avoidance pattern.

The Big Fifty bucked into his shoulder, but in his nervousness Bolton had jerked the trigger, pulling his shot. He was thumbing his next round into the breech when a second arrow thwapped into the packhorse—missing Danford by mere inches.

The next second, all hell broke loose.

This time the exploding arrow had scored a direct hit on the ammo belts. All of a sudden Kristen could have sworn it was Fourth of July on Broadway—except that these weren't harmless firecrackers exploding in chain reaction, but live, lethal rounds.

Danford, pale as new linen, ducked for his life as he raced back to his horse. Rounds whizzed everywhere, making the air hum like a beehive.

"Forget about Fargo or he'll blow us to smithereens with them arrows!" he ordered. "And leave the packhorse!"

He fairly flew into his saddle, grabbed the leadline to Kristen's horse, and started toward Whistling Rock. But Fargo had cleverly angled perfectly to cut them off. The best escape route now was toward the east.

New hope surged within Kristen. Every time she was on the verge of giving up, this tough-as-nails Trailsman wouldn't let her. And every time these thugs knocked him down, he came up fighting even harder.

The Ovaro would have literally killed himself before giving up if Fargo hadn't reined him in to blow. That final assault, Fargo realized, had almost been the decisive strike. But Bolton and Danford hadn't been pushing their mounts nearly as hard as he had, nor as long, and soon they had opened up a lead.

However, Fargo had accomplished his immediate goal. Once again his prey were on the run in open country. He stopped to rescue the frightened but unharmed packhorse, ripping the flaming load off just in time. Fargo let the Ovaro rest while he picketed the packhorse for later collection.

He couldn't help a little grin at his luck—*sheer* luck in striking the ammo stores. Danford and Bolton had hopped and danced like hounds with their tails on fire. He only hoped none of those rounds had wounded Kristen.

He knew this was no time to let up. The best time to press pursuit was when your enemy was nerve-rattled. Fargo paused only long enough to spell the Ovaro, meantime stripping off his tack to dry the stallion with a singed blanket pulled off of the packhorse.

He bore due east, eyes in constant motion. Although this was mostly barren, open country dotted with animal fossils, there were enough rock clusters to pose a danger. He had two exploding arrows left. But these unique inventions had done their job. Now Fargo loosened the riding thong on his Colt and slid it out of the holster, keeping it to hand. The next attack, when it came, would be at close quarters.

And it came quicker than he expected.

He had already skirted several clusters of rock, noticing that the tracks he was following bypassed them. The ground hereabouts was mostly dry pan, but an experienced eye could detect disturbed pebbles and displaced stones. Finally, the trail entered directly into a larger than usual clutch of rocks.

As Fargo drew closer, the Ovaro's ears twitched forward. The stallion had caught a scent.

Fargo threw off, not bothering with hobbles—the Ovaro was trained to stand still when the reins were thrown forward. Thumbing back his hammer, Fargo moved cautiously into the shadow of the first outlying rocks.

He had expected the set-to to happen farther in. But he immediately walked into a classic pincers trap.

Quick as a striking snake, Dakota Danford popped up from cover on the left flank, his Smith & Wesson magazine pistol spitting flame. Fargo's hair-trigger reflexes saved him, for he tucked and rolled just in the nick of time to duck the bullet.

Fargo's Colt jumped into his hand and fired. Danford, a look of stunned disbelief on his face, folded dead to the ground. Unfortunately, Fargo was in no position to turn around quick enough when, from the corner of his eye, he saw a grinning Red Bolton emerge from cover, six-shooter at the ready.

A gun spoke its deadly piece, and Skye Fargo waited for the slamming jolt as he finally met death. But that jolt never came. Instead, Red Bolton took two staggering steps, wobbled on his feet, then collapsed, heels scratching the dirt a few times before he gave up the ghost.

Stunned, Fargo watched Kristen emerge behind Bolton. Blue wisps of smoke still curled from the derringer in her hand.

Fargo saw her staring at the dead man. When he realized she was going to faint, he scrambled to his feet just in time to catch her before she collapsed. He let her down gently to the ground, cradling her head.

155

She recovered a few moments later and gave him a weak smile. "Well, Mr. Fargo, I guess, by your manly Code of the West, I'm a back-shooter now?"

He grinned and shook his head. "Nope. You can't back-shoot a back-shooter. He lost all rights in the matter."

"I guess this city girl is learning. I hope I did the right thing back in the cave by igniting that magnesium powder? Maybe you had a better plan, and I messed it all up."

Fargo laughed, swiping at the loose tendrils of blond hair covering her eyes. In this light, they were a soft, hazy blue.

"You might say the whole crazy scheme was a flash in the pan," he punned. "But so happens I had no plan, so you saved those kids *and* me. Matter fact, city girl, this makes twice you saved my life."

She gave him a sexy up-and-under look, batting her lashes. "Then you should be grateful. And after I've bathed somewhere and rested up a bit, I'll expect you to show your gratitude."

Fargo sighed like a put-upon martyr. "A man must do his duty, no matter how pleasant."

Kristen finally got her bath later that evening when the two riders, leading a string of horses, made camp in a sheltered copse beside the White River.

All Fargo could offer her was a lump of yellow lye soap he pulled from the bottom of a pannier. Both of them stripped, in the golden light of a full moon, and sudsed each other in the chilly but bracing river. Then Kristen scrubbed the dirt from her clothing and hung it on tree branches to dry in the breeze.

Skye settled back in the lush grass of the river bank, admiring her naked form as she worked. There was an old joke in the woman-scarce West: most men had to settle for anything that got off the train. Well, this little dolly-bird had indeed been pulled off the train, but her beauty was anything but a joke.

And she was definitely the type who "jiggled" when she walked, he thought, watching her heavy, pendant breasts swaying as she approached him.

"Here, you dropped this awhile back," he said, handing her the lacquered straw hat with its bright blue ribbon and gay ostrich feather. "Sorry the feather got a little bent, it's been riding in my saddle pannier."

"My hat!" she exclaimed. "I lost it when the train was derailed."

He nodded, pulling her down into the grass beside him. "Once I smelled that honeysuckle on it, I knew I had to return it."

She studied him, her hair tumbling loose like a spun-gold waterfall. "I've never met a man like you. Some men spend so much time alone they don't think and act like the majority."

"That bother you?"

"An independent man as handsome as you," she assured him, "bothers *any* red-blooded woman. It's our nature to acquire and tame. Aren't you interested in putting down roots somewhere?"

"Roots? Cupcake, if I stay rooted too long in one place, I get holed-up fever. My feet are already starting to itch. Time to move on."

Her heart-shaped lips formed a pout. "The big, tough Trailsman! All man and covered with hard bark. If he can't eat it, drink it, or bed it, he throws it away. Oh, why do I always fall for you hard-to-hold men?"

He pulled her over on top of him, one hand slipping between her satiny inner thighs to part them. "There, there, that's a tough old soldier," he teased her, sliding his curving length into her slippery sheath. "I ain't so hard to hold right this minute, am I?"

She gasped at the pleasant surprise of his entry.

"Oh, not at all, but you *are* hard," she moaned, her hips starting to buck. "So nice and hard!"

Within thirty seconds, she was panting like an express pony. Fargo slipped his hands behind her ass and cupped both round, firm cheeks, guiding her up and down his length.

"Oh, Lord, Skye! You . . . that . . . it feels so . . . oh, oh, *oh*! Like that, Skye, yes, YES! Harder, Skye! Faster, faster, don't stop, don't ever—oh, ahh, ahh, ANHH!"

With a powerful shudder that left dozens of aftershocks in her belly, she peaked, squeezing him over and over with her love muscle and bringing him across the Great Divide with her. Her peevish mood was over. And for the rest of that night, Fargo left her no more time for complaints.

157

17

"Well, gents, there goes the rat catcher," Owen Maitland announced. "Now Bear Creek has got a chance to start fresh."

He, Skye Fargo, Slappy Hupenbecker, and young Danny Ford stood in the open doorway of the livery stable, watching the unusual activity out on the street. Owen and several others in town had supplied a complete list of Red Bolton's "deputies." Now they were all being hauled off in two tumbleweed wagons, as prison vans were called, to stand trial in the territorial court convening at Fort Laramie. Their number included Nash Johnson. Reece Jenkins, the only other surviving member of the Danford gang, had already been formally charged with murder, kidnapping, and extortion.

"Slade Pendergast has a U.S. marshal already on the way," Owen added. "A former Texas Ranger he handpicked himself. No more of these vigilance committees."

"Good thing, too," Fargo said. "Now that you got all these new young citizens to protect."

Because of everything those twelve waifs from New York had endured together, the railroad and the town of Bear Creek had agreed to place them in good homes in the Bear Creek area—close enough together that they would all grow up friends and neighbors. Even little Ginny, according to a report Kristen had sent Skye, had come out of her emotional shell and was once again smiling and talking.

"Them ain't the only ones need protecting," Slappy chimed in. "Believe you me, Danny boy here is a rich man now. And a hero into the bargain."

Once the full details came out in the newspapers, Danny

had indeed been hailed as a local hero for riding up that dangerous bluff with Fargo. The grateful railroad barons (who, after all, had saved one hundred thousand dollars *and* a nasty blow to their image) had given the boy five hundred dollars—a tidy sum at a time when the average worker supported his family on about forty dollars a month.

Danny flushed. "Ahh, horse feathers. Mr. Fargo got paid ten times that amount. And *he* done all the work."

"Except," Owen cut in, "that I have it, from a reliable newspaper source, that Skye has quietly distributed that five thousand dollars to the families who took in the kids."

"Oh, I kept a hundred dollars for myself," Fargo corrected him. "That'll stake me for months."

He headed toward the stall where the Ovaro stood waiting, well fed and rested.

"That air reliable newspaper source," Slappy repeated. "Wouldn't happen to be Kristen McKenna, would it?"

Owen grinned. "In the creamy flesh. She's been sent to Omaha. The *New York Herald* has set her up as their first official Far West Bureau. In fact, she's already filed her first story. It's called 'A Gentleman Unafraid.' Care to hear a snippet of it, Skye?"

Fargo, busy centering his saddle, nodded. "Sure. I ain't never read her work."

Owen pulled a sheet of newsprint from his vest pocket and unfolded it. He read in a clear, strong voice: " 'By no means is Skye Fargo an unfriendly man, just "standoffish" as one of his vanquished enemies described him. Fargo likes to pick his own company or go without it, as he pleases. Civil to most men, servile to none. Some distant secret of his own shows, sometimes, in those penetrating blue eyes. But like most strong men who survive daily on a dangerous frontier, he lives in the present moment. Ever alert, knowing the next fight is always coming, and determined to win it, for he is a true gentleman knight in buckskins.' "

"Well, I'll be et fir a tater!" Slappy exclaimed. "Skye, that describes you right down to the ground. That little gal writes as good as she looks."

"Sounds a mite flowery," was all Fargo said as he mounted.

"Where you headed, Mr. Fargo?" Danny asked.

"Oh, just trailing the sun, Danny. Trailing the sun. . . ."

Fargo nodded to all three of his friends. Then, reins in hand once again, the Trailsman nudged the Ovaro out into the street.

But he didn't get far before a pretty sight arrested his progress: Dusty Robinson, that peart little dime-a-dance gal, stood at the end of the alley which led to her door. She wore a simple but flattering blue cotton dress. A woven-reed basket depended from one arm.

Fargo tipped his hat. "Dusty, how you getting along?"

"I heard you were leaving today," she replied. "I just wanted to clear up something before you go. When I told you I only *dance* with men for money? I forgot to add that it's different when there's no money involved. If you take my meaning?"

She flushed at her own boldness, and Fargo felt his lips tugging into a grin. "Well now . . . is that an invitation of sorts?"

She nodded. "It most certainly is. This basket's filled with all sorts of good food. Would you like to come in for a . . . meal?"

A line from Kristen's article came back to Fargo now: *But like most men who survive daily on a dangerous frontier, he lives in the present moment.* Hell, he couldn't make that famous reporter out to be a liar, could he?

"I'd admire to," Fargo replied, swinging down and leading his stallion into the alley.

LOOKING FORWARD!

**The following is the opening
section of the next novel in the exciting
Trailsman series from Signet:**

THE TRAILSMAN #263
Arkansas Assault

*Tillman, Arkansas, 1858—
A madman's lust for sex and murder of
the most twisted kind.*

Fargo eased his big Ovaro stallion behind a copse of pine
trees and started watching the stage road with the lake blue
eyes that had seen so much in his lifetime.

He was used to bounty hunters trailing him. Fargo had
helped out enough people in his days to amass a fair share
of enemies. And these enemies included several crooked
lawmen. Because they were afraid to face him down themselves, they put out WANTED posters and slapped some
mighty big rewards on them.

So every once in a while a bounty hunter keen on earn-
ing a rep for being the one who killed the Trailsman
showed up out of nowhere. Sure, the money was a factor,
but so was the prestige of bringing down Skye Fargo.

Such an opportunist—a gunny and sometimes bounty
hunter named Jeb Adams—had been following him for

three days and nights now. Fargo hadn't paid him much attention at first. Every time he hit a town, Fargo managed to find a place to sleep where Adams couldn't get him. Not that Fargo took stupid chances. He slept on his back, his Colt and his Henry right beside him in case Adams got lucky and came crawling into the room in the middle of the night.

But last night Adams had done something that turned Skye Fargo into a mortal enemy. He'd tried to poison Fargo's stallion.

Only the quick thinking of the old black man who slept in the livery at night saved Fargo's horse. The old man had awakened to the sounds of Adams—not exactly a graceful man—sneaking into the livery, then watched from the shadows as Adams mixed a powdery substance into the animal's feed bag that was brimming with oats.

The old man knew not to take Adams on. Adams would kill him in a flash. No, the old man wisely waited until Adams left, and then he went up and grabbed the feed bag. He waited until Skye Fargo showed up the next morning. He told Fargo what had happened and what the late-night visitor had looked like. Anybody who knew Fargo knew what his stallion meant to him. A wandering and solitary man like Fargo had few friends. It was only natural for his horse to become the best among them.

Fargo's first impulse was to go find the sonofabitch and shoot him on the spot. The problem was, Fargo didn't know any of the local lawmen. Even if it was a fair fight, the sheriff here might decide that Fargo should be charged anyway. For a man whose only guiding light was the sun and the stars—he could go anywhere, anytime he wanted—the thought of prison, even for a few days, was the ugliest thought of all.

So Fargo decided to meet Adams outside the jurisdiction of the small Arkansas town he found himself in.

He made himself as obvious as he could this morning, taking an early breakfast at the local café, and loudly greeting the day crew at the livery as they arrived for work.

Two or three times, he spotted Adams glowering at him

from various positions. He could imagine Adams's surprise and fury when he realized that the stallion was still alive.

Adams was doing everything Skye Fargo wanted him to.

It didn't take Adams long to show up, either.

About ten minutes after Fargo had taken up his hiding place behind the pines, here came his good friend Adams.

The fierce Old Testament beard, the stained buckskins, the ancient and once white hat, the blue glass eye glaring from the right socket, Adams was a hard man to mistake for any other. And that went not just for his physical appearance but for the way he did his business, too. He was well-known for not giving his bounty any chance to go peacefully. A lot of times, he broke in on them during the night somewhere and shot them in cold blood. Sometimes the wife and children of the wanted man had to watch the man die right in front of them. He'd even been accused, though not convicted, of raping some of the wives after killing off their menfolk.

One hell of a nice fella was Jeb Adams.

Fargo waited in the steamy midday heat wave—the temperature was on its way to one hundred degrees—swatting away various mosquitoes, flies, bees, and other flying things he wasn't sure he'd ever laid eyes on before. Arkansas was one of the muggiest, hottest places he'd ever been.

Fargo waited until Adams passed him on the road. Then he quickly swung down from the stallion, grabbing his Henry and stepping out onto the road so Adams could see him.

"That's far enough, Adams. Stop right there or I'll put three bullets in your back. The way you do with the men you hunt."

Adams was smart enough to stop his horse but not smart enough to keep his mouth shut. "Well, well, Skye Fargo. We finally meet up."

"You tried to poison my horse."

Adams, a huge man, had a huge and raspy laugh. "I believe I did, now that I think about it."

"I'm taking you in and having the sheriff arrest you."

This time, the laugh was even fuller, deeper. "I guess you haven't figured that town out yet, have you?"

"Turn toward me nice and slow with your hands up."

Adams did what Fargo demanded. When Fargo finally saw his face, he realized that the man was sneering at him.

"I said to put your hands up."

"I don't think you'd want to shoot me, Fargo."

"Yeah? Why not?"

The sneer widened. "Like I said, I don't think you figured out that town yet."

"Meaning what?"

"Meaning that the sheriff there is my cousin. Meaning that if anything happens to me, he's gonna come right after you. I told him who I was chasing. He said he'd help me get you if I'd split the reward money." The laugh again. And the almost luminous, somehow crazed dark eyes stared, at Fargo, in the shadows cast by the brim of the hat. "But my cousin Bobby Wayne? He's just as mercenary as I am, Fargo. He'd help me get you all right—then he'd come up with some reason for killin' me. All nice and legal, you understand. And then he'd keep all that reward money for himself." He shook his head in mock grief. "Terrible thing when a man can't even trust his own cousin."

"Get down off your horse."

"Guess you didn't hear me about my cousin Bobby Wayne."

"I'm not worried about Bobby Wayne. I'm taking you to the next town on."

"That'd be Tillman, I think. They've got quite a Fourth of July celebration there, I'm told. In fact, that's where I'm headed now. Old friend of mine—did a lot of work for him in my time—he offered me a job. I'm thinkin' about takin' it. Thought I'd get some cash pulled together before I got there. That's where you came in, Fargo. You've got a nice price on your head."

"Down off the horse—after you pitch that six-gun and that rifle down here first."

Adams shook his head in mock grief again. "Awful thing that you don't trust me, Fargo."

Fargo used his Colt to put a bullet right through the

highest point of Adams's battered, greasy old hat. The hat didn't sail off, just slanted to the right on Adams's large head.

"Nice shootin', Fargo."

"The Colt first. Then the Henry."

When Adams moved his right hand too quickly toward his holster, Fargo put another bullet close to him, about half an inch from Adams's gun hand. "Slow and easy, Adams. Don't give me any excuse to kill you. Because I'll take it."

"I was just doin' what you told me, Fargo." You couldn't see his sneer now but you could certainly hear it in his voice.

Fargo watched him carefully.

Adams slid the Colt out from the holster, dangled it daintily by its handle, and then dropped it into the sunbaked dust of the road. He looked as if he'd been handling a piece of feces. Giving in to the Trailsman was obviously not good for the bounty hunter's pride.

"Now the rifle."

"You're a hard man, Fargo." Mocking him, of course.

"Just throw it down, Adams."

And then it happened.

Fargo had to give the man credit. He was able to drop the rifle to the dusty road with one hand while at the same time, with the other hand, draw a small revolver from somewhere in the folds of his buckskins.

Adams got the first shot off, dropping from his horse an instant after.

Fargo threw himself to the ground. There wasn't time to get back behind the pines. He rolled away from Adams's horse just as Adams started firing at him. Adams was down on one knee, getting his shots away from under the belly of his animal.

"Looks like I'm givin' the orders now, Fargo."

He clipped off two more shots, making Fargo roll behind some brush on the roadside. The tangled growth gave Fargo the only cover he could find. "Give up now, Adams. Go in peaceful."

"Hell, man, you're gonna be dead in a couple minutes. I'll be taking you in. To a funeral home."

Adams must have believed his own bragging because he now stepped out in front of his horse and aimed his six-shooter right at the brush where Fargo was hiding. He squeezed off his shot.

To a bystander, this moment would have looked awfully damned odd. Here it was Adams who'd done the shooting. But it was also Adams who, an instant later, clutched his chest as a flower-shaped redness appeared on the front of his buckskin shirt. And then he struck a pose like a bad dancer, his limbs all seeming to point in different directions. His small revolver tumbled from his hand. His hand, like the rest of his body, remained in this awkward position for another long moment. And then the huge man collapsed, the ground trembling as his body met it with real force and speed.

Not much doubt that Jeb Adams was dead.

Fargo had fired at the exact instant Adams had. Adams's gun made more noise than Fargo's. So an observer would have heard only Adams's shot. The difference between the two shots was that Fargo's had hit home, right in the heart. Adams's had gone wild.

Fargo picked himself up, dusted himself off, and went over and haunched down next to the corpse. He checked wrist and neck pulse points to be sure the man was really dead.

Getting him up on his horse's back wasn't easy. It wasn't just the considerable weight. It was the form death had twisted Adams into. He was hard to get a hold of. But finally the Trailsman was able to carry him over to the horse and throw him across the saddle. Fargo took a couple of deep breaths, flicked away some gnats who'd been dining on his sweat.

He went through the dead man's saddlebags.

Adams had a couple of dozen WANTED posters. If the reward had been increased on a particular man, he'd noted this in pencil at the bottom of the poster. There was a notarized letter informing Adams that his divorce had gone through. According to a second letter in the same envelope—a bitter letter from Adams's ex-wife—Adams had been a terrible husband and a worse father, a man who had embarrassed and humiliated his wife in every way possible, including a "tryst" with a woman down the street. The letter was from Saint Louis and was two years old.

There was another letter from a man named Noah Tillman. It read:

> *I hope this finds you well, Jeb. Though I'm troubled by a damned skin rash from time to time, I'm doing pretty well. My empire is making more money than ever. I say this knowing that it sounds as if I'm bragging. But hell, it's the truth. And you helped make it that way. Those two "eliminations" you did for me were important.*
>
> *You were also helpful in setting up my little project on Skeleton Key. That's why I'm sending you this letter. I hope you'll be able to join me this July 4. I'll take you to the Key and show you how to have some real fun. I don't think there's anything like it in these United States. In fact, I'm sure there isn't.*
>
> *I hope to see you then.*

The brief letter told Fargo that Adams had been doing two jobs at once—tracking Fargo and traveling to his rich friend's place. The word "eliminations" clued Fargo in that Jeb Adams had probably been a hired killer as well as a bounty hunter. This Noah Tillman had apparently been a customer. Rich men frequently needed to have business rivals killed. Hired killing was a lucrative business if you were good at it. And Fargo didn't doubt that Adams had been *damned* good at it.

Fargo jammed the letter from Noah Tillman in his pocket. He'd have a surprise for this Noah Tillman. Jeb Adams was going to show up, all right.

Dead.

No other series has this much historical action!

THE TRAILSMAN

Available wherever books are sold, or
to order call: 1-800-788-6262